CELESTIAL WHISPERS

DAVE MANAV

I am deeply thankful <u>to my family</u> for their unwavering support and encouragement throughout my journey. I would also like to express my heartfelt gratitude to <u>BHAVIKA PANT</u> for her invaluable assistance and belief in me every step of the way.

I have my Sincere thanks to <u>Pushti Parekh</u> and <u>Parth Parmar.</u>

Contents

Contents

Preface

I'm a 20-year-old student and aspiring writer from Gujarat, India, exploring the world of storytelling. Since my early years, I've been captivated by the power of storywriting. Despite the demands of student life, I find comfort in crafting narratives that resonate deeply with readers. Much of my work, including my novella "Celestial Whispers," is based on true events. One of the central stories, Mr. Hermit's story, is inspired by my grandfather. Through his story, I want to share a message with everyone: your mistakes and your life are meaningful, even if you are suffering. At the end of the day, we are all just particles in this vast universe, and each of our stories matters. Currently, I am navigating the realms of academia and creativity, striving to balance both while telling stories that connect and inspire.

Prologue

Everything we witness is real. The question arises repeatedly, eventually becoming a habit to ignore the one thing connecting us to celestial matters.

Meet Dave, a character lost in thought. His mind often wanders into unknown realms. Despite following a daily routine like everyone else, his mind sets him apart.

Driven by curiosity, Dave decides to explore a mysterious mountain known to no one. His friend Lucy, whose father oversees the forest department, possesses data on those who ventured up the mountain—a discovery Dave makes while satisfying his curiosity.

What mysteries will he uncover? Who is the Hermit, and why does he share his story, urging Dave to learn more?

This novella promises a valuable lesson, reminding us that no story is without purpose. Every tale holds significance.

CHAPTER ONE

An Unfamiliar Similarity

Where am I?

Everything has changed here, according to time, and I cannot even expect everything to be the same here. I'd be foolish to expect that.

But it's like I have come here many times, I belong here. And still, I am unable to recognize what I am seeing now. I am unable to catch vibes here; it is different from what it used to be.

Everything that I am seeing here is as it was before. Everything is placed in its original place, and nothing has changed at all, not a single thing. The only thing that has changed here is **ME.**

At times, it seems as if we're caught in a never-ending cycle. Our physical presence remains stagnant while our thoughts wander off, far from any notion of moving forward. It's like we're immersed in a complex storyline, so engrossing that we lose track of everything else. Our minds become consumed by these narratives, where every event unfolds rapidly, <u>almost in the blink of an eye.</u>

CHAPTER TWO

Forest Whispers

Hello class and good morning to one and all present here. My name is DAVE, and today I am going to give a brief presentation about evolution. An evolution that has been conveyed to us through mythology and modern science. In today's presentation, I will discuss how life is created according to both aspects, and I will also connect our understanding of evolution as seen in mythology and modern science. What I am about to share will compel you to rethink many different scenarios. So, without further delay, let me begin with where life begins...

(After one hour of boredom or excitement.)

Hello DAVE, your presentation was awesome. After listening to the connection between both aspects, I was stunned. I had many questions about this topic, and more have arisen after hearing your presentation and it multiplied after hearing you. I also want to know more about astrology and the connection between our universes with others. I want to learn about the theory of the multiverse. I have some questions regarding philosophy and dimensions. After observing and listening to your presentation, I sense that you have more to share, and you possess some interesting knowledge about these particular subjects. So, I would like to discuss everything you knows, if not today, then perhaps someday.

Tell me about your schedule so we can decide when and where to meet.

Class rep, LUCY. New student to our town. A girl full of ambition, questions, mysteries, and maturity. Whenever I look at her, I see a reflection of my own thoughts. She only speaks when she finds it necessary and worth. I feel she is the only one whose vibes resonated with mine, as we both are dark individuals. People like us don't care much about others. But regardless, what should I say to her question? My schedule is quite busy these days.

What are you doing this weekend, LUCY? Because I have to stay at our university for long this weekend, and as I am also involved in my extracurricular activities. I have participated in more than two activities, so I won't be free until the weekend as I have to prepare for that.

How about Saturday at 5:00 PM?

Um, yeah, sounds good. No worries from my side. So, suggest a place you like.

DAVE, there is a good café near my home. It has just opened last month and has a unique HALLOWEEN theme. You'll definitely like it.

(Her home is 10km away from the city. Absolutely, I am not going to allow myself to go there. No chance. She has questions, yeah, definitely a good thing, but making someone travel for that is not fair. She is mature enough to understand everything, so she should at least understand that it's not fair.)

Okay, LUCY. See you on Saturday. I'll be on time.

(WTF! What are you doing, DAVE? You are the most foolish person in the universe. A minute ago, you are refusing to go there. And now you want to go because a mysterious girl wants you to be there. Where's your self-respect that you were talking about?)

UFF, these goddamn hormones.

(After 3 days)

I kicked the bike and started the journey. The route from my place to LUCY's place takes approximately 40 minutes and surpasses through a forested area. Forests have always thrilled me because of the trees and the cold breeze. I enjoy places where human reach is limited, where I can observe many things, and where I can contemplate my surroundings.

As I reached the middle of the way, I was thankful for my hormones. I really liked the place and the route. It's dangerous to roam alone here, but I'm drawn to such places, covered in woods, where sunlight barely touches the road. Seeing footways that connect the road to the forest ignites my curiosity about who has gone there and what they have done, and how many have visited this place before me and for what reason.

(After 55 minutes)

I stood at the main gate of her home. Her home is huge and covered with trees and a male German shepherd who is looking at me with his killer eyes. There aren't any other residents nearby, making the place seem kind of scary, plus her dog. As I recalled the day, she was wearing a white top with dark blue jeans and her flowing hair make her a worth person to see. When I gave her a flirty compliment, she smiled.

She just smiled? Wow.

We drove through the cold, and after nearly 5 minutes, we reached a café and grabbed two cups of tea. As we sipped our tea, I posed a question to her while enjoying the sunset view which was so mesmerizing. LUCY, tell me, **What Is the Purpose of Our Life?**

She took her time, looking at the sunset & sipping her tea: To have **"NO REGRETS"** after we die and to fulfill our **KARMA**. That's what I think. Now you tell me, what's your answer?

As she asked me, I filled my lungs with one long breath and released it, saying: I don't think there is any purpose to our lives. Just as I asked you a perceptual question, there may be many answers, but I don't believe there is any purpose to our lives in this illusionary world. While she was pondering my question, I asked her another:

LUCY, I believe in some energy, whatever it may be. Maybe God for some. One random day, I wondered, WHY DID GOD CREATED US? We call them a supreme energy. So why did they need to create us? What was their motive in making us, creating us, when they can do everything on their own?

She looked amazed and thoughtful for a few minutes once again. I started hearing the sound of a moving breeze. After a minute or two, she replied with a sad look:

MAYBE BECAUSE **"EVEN OUR CREATOR ALSO FELT LONELINESS".**

The answer shocked and amazed me. I think maybe she has experienced the same thing, or maybe she is mature enough to understand things.

And we stood there with a silence between us.

LUCY, I think we should leave now. When I came here, I didn't realize that your home would take much time. But it has already been an hour since I arrived. So, it is better to talk less this time. We'll definitely meet someday.

She agreed by replying: I think it's better to go because it is already dusk, and it would be better if you reach before night. We left the place. And don't know why, but I have always been one who doesn't like goodbyes. We all have to face that part of life in every step of growing.

Again, the same route through the forest. If someone were left within the silence of the forest, they would surely encounter the unknown danger by which they are unaware of. Mental danger or fear.

(After a while of driving)

We reached at LUCY's home. We shook hands, and I said: It's good to have you as my company today, and sorry because I didn't get a chance to know about your thoughts and your questions. We also didn't have a long discussion, so it's better if we meet next weekend if possible.

I left as soon as she said: Sure, I would like to. (We exchanged phone numbers). She said to give her a call if we don't have the chance to meet on weekends.

(Is she thinking of meeting every weekend? LOL.)

The route is creepier than before, but I am a little excited this time. I always liked cold and dark vibes. I truly enjoy this route. But the weird thing about this route is (it feels like someone is following me, stalking me). I don't know why I like dark and psychopathic things. I am a nyctophile person. It gives me thrilling vibes, but this time, it was a creepy atmosphere.

After riding for a few minutes, I found a way through the woods. I told myself to go there someday because the route is creepy, and creepy things are a lot of fun to explore. I have noticed since childhood that the things which are creepy has not always been that way; something must have made that place creepy, and maybe that something is time or dark energy. And I was curious about the way I was seeing in the lone way while having glance at first sight. Where there is not much of human interference, how there be a way?

(After I reached home)

I had dinner and went upstairs to my room. I opened my window and felt the fresh breeze enter my body. Then, I did what I was supposed to do at night; I resumed reading. I have been reading a classic horror book since long, and expect to finish it within a week. I also liked reading books of different genres and I choose different genres according to my mood and craving to improve and increase my knowledge. I read because books help me find our fantasy and know myself better.

And at last, I slept.

CHAPTER THREE

Curiosity

Another morning, and instead of heading to my university, I veered towards the path through the woods that caught my eye yesterday while riding home after meeting LUCY.

Sometimes, the urge to explore things overwhelms us,

The craving to uncover the fantasy behind it,

The risk to understand it.

(After a 20-minute drive)

I parked on that isolated road and started walking towards the way which is lonely and I feel like the way has its eyes over me. The trees are denser and the air is getting thicker as I continued walking. As I ventured deeper into the woods, I sensed the forest thickening, the air growing heavier, and the surroundings getting darker and quieter. The silence was unsettling and my mind gets disturbance. In a world where our brains are accustomed to constant stimulation, moments of absolute quiet can unsettle the mind by overthinking thought. Even now, when we try to be alone, there's always someone around us that's what we feel. But the prospect of being truly alone in a place like this—a forest or anywhere with minimal human interference was haunted. Despite that, the allure of experiencing something new, of collecting stories, drove me forward.

I walked for over 5 kilometers, contemplating two possible outcomes: 1) Turn back home due to the long journey, or 2) Keep walking until I find something or make a memorable discovery. As a traveler at heart, I opted for the latter.

(30 minutes later)

I stumbled upon mountains adorned with towering trees, sheltering them from sunlight, with water flowing gracefully through the landscape. The sight took my breath away, which was already labored from the trek. It was a scene unlike any other I had witnessed—beautiful yet tinged with an eerie vibe. The dark forest held an air of danger, contrasting sharply with the serene exterior. Amidst it all, a colossal mountain stood proudly, dominating the horizon.

To my left and right, I noticed board placed at a distance, piquing my curiosity. As I approached, I saw a DANGER sign, its ominous red hue stirring both fear within me. What events had unfolded in this abandoned place to warrant such a warning? In movies and series, we often see humans thriving in the forest, but the reality of the forest experience is daunting with uncertainty. Yet, to achieve something, one must dare to take risks. One should be the initiator, one should be a person to break the limit.

However, this time, I decided against it. I had a home to return and being alone in this unknown place was beginning to unnerve me. Besides, no one knew of my whereabouts, and I felt a bit of fear creeping in. I resolved to inquire about this place from LUCY, as it was near her home.

CHAPTER FOUR

Mountain of Mystery

Another morning, and instead of heading to my university, I veered towards the path through the woods that caught my eye yesterday while riding home after meeting LUCY.

Sometimes, the urge to explore things overwhelms us,
The craving to uncover the fantasy behind it,
The risk to understand it.

(After a 20-minute drive)

I parked on that isolated road and started walking towards the way which is lonely and I feel like the way has its eyes over me. The trees are denser and the air is getting thicker as I continued walking. As I ventured deeper into the woods, I sensed the forest thickening, the air growing heavier, and the surroundings getting darker and quieter. The silence was unsettling and my mind gets disturbance. In a world where our brains are accustomed to constant stimulation, moments of absolute quiet can unsettle the mind by overthinking thought. Even now, when we try to be alone, there's always someone around us that's what we feel. But the prospect of being truly alone in a place like this—a forest or anywhere with minimal human interference was haunted. Despite that, the allure of experiencing something new, of collecting stories, drove me forward.

I walked for over 5 kilometers, contemplating two possible outcomes: 1) Turn back home due to the long journey, or 2) Keep walking until I find something or make a memorable discovery. As a traveler at heart, I opted for the latter.

(30 minutes later)

I stumbled upon mountains adorned with towering trees, sheltering them from sunlight, with water flowing gracefully through the landscape. The sight took my breath away, which was already labored from the trek. It was a scene unlike any other I had witnessed—beautiful yet tinged with an eerie vibe. The dark forest held an air of danger, contrasting sharply with the serene exterior. Amidst it all, a colossal mountain stood proudly, dominating the horizon.

To my left and right, I noticed board placed at a distance, piquing my curiosity. As I approached, I saw a DANGER sign, its ominous red hue stirring both fear within me. What events had unfolded in this abandoned place to warrant such a warning? In movies and series, we often see humans thriving in the forest, but the reality of the forest experience is daunting with uncertainty. Yet, to achieve something, one must dare to take risks. One should be the initiator, one should be a person to break the limit.

However, this time, I decided against it. I had a home to return and being alone in this unknown place was beginning to unnerve me. Besides, no one knew of my whereabouts, and I felt a bit of fear creeping in. I resolved to inquire about this place from LUCY, as it was near her home.

CHAPTER FIVE

Unveiling Secrets

There is no place on the internet where we can know about the mountain; there was no article related to it, not even a single detail. And this thing is getting on my nerves. After we tried to find it everywhere we possibly could, Lucy told me about her dad's folder (as a forest governor, they do have records regarding the places they are in). She wants to dare to see it because she thinks she may find some lead about the mountain, which I think is creepy. There must be some record as that place is not that bad to ignore. It can definitely be used as a tourist spot or picnic place, as per what I think. I've never been this curious before. What is it that humans always find weird about things?

Why don't we just leave things as they are?

We know that we aren't going to get any answers from the world about the other universe and celestial beings. We are not even getting answers of this world still why humans want to know everything? Human's even wants to know what their neighbors are doing in day to day life. This is such a drag. So, I let my instincts do their work.

(After a day)

Lucy got the names, and when I viewed those names, I was so goddamn shocked. The name written on the page, which Lucy clicked a photo of on her mobile phone really shocked me. There were many names written on it. I was literally shocked because the name written on the page was also includes name of my parents. Lucy told me that this one is the recent one, and she was unable to find previous list. And it was a relief. After reading their names, I was silent for so long until Lucy asked me about my instant stillness. I avoided answering the reality because I was literally unaware of my parents until now, and even now, I am unaware of everything. What happened on the mountain that only a few reputed people can go there? I didn't share that with Lucy; she might have already noticed. I was then about to leave, so I told Lucy to leave this matter, as it was kind of a waste of time anyway.

As I recall, its 10 p.m. when I reached home, and both my parents were sitting and talking with each other. I interrupted them and asked, "Hey dad, do you know anything about the mountain which is beautiful and still no one visits? I went there yesterday, and I'm so curious about the danger sign boarded up there. Is there something suspicious there?" The reply I got from my dad was, "Why don't you find it by yourself?" After hearing an unexpected answer from my dad, I went up to my room, thinking about what just happened. I think I was expecting something more of a drama, mysteries and fear. But it was all just unexpected. My dad just gave me permission to climb the mountain where there is a board of danger. Something just doesn't smell right.

Into the Unknown

It was 6 in the morning when I packed my bag last night and went straight to the mountain where I was not allowed to go, but strangely, I was allowed to. I started walking until I saw the danger board, marking the beginning of my unexpected journey. The way was full of trekking, darkness, and cold air, as it seemed from a bird's eye view. The closer I got to the mountain, the thinner the air felt, as forest areas have purer air compared to cities. The more I walked, the less I could see due to the increasing fog. (It was like I was nearing Dracula's castle. I joked myself by saying this.)

After a few hours of walking in this terrifying place, I found a cave. Yes, a cave. Everything feels so magical when I recall it from the past, but indeed, the present is more magical; we just don't realize it in the moment. **Our present acts like wine; the older it gets, the better it tastes.** Like every human instinct, I didn't went in at once. I picked up a few stones and rocks, and had my trekking pole with me in case I needed to defend myself. I began throwing rocks into the cave to check for any wild animals. When I received no response, I moved inside.

I think the cave was about 500m long, so I started walking down. I walked until the end, and I found something amazing - a water cave.

The scene was terrifically amazing and calming because, first of all, I had reached here all alone, which I thought was both foolish and perhaps a great decision. But the scene I was witnessing was so satisfying. I sat there for a long time, putting my legs in the water. Sometimes I think that the places humans don't know about are the best to visit. The vibe of this place was totally different, until I heard footsteps. As soon as I heard them, I hid behind a huge stone. All I saw was an incoming hermit or a monk—a hermit fetching water from the water cave. There are always humans whose aura is so strong, like this hermit's aura. I felt safe just looking at him, so I automatically started walking towards him to meet him. I thought for a second that this might be a trap or maybe I should not trust him. But I was attracted to him like a magnetic field, like he was a magnet attracting magnetic dust. Or was I being hypnotized?

Whatever the case, I was walking towards the hermit, who didn't seem to know I was coming. While fetching water, the hermit spoke, "What took you so long reaching me?" I was stunned by his expressions and words. It was like he had been waiting for me for a long time. He fetched his water and told me to follow him. He was taking me somewhere out of human reach; well, obviously, he's a hermit (is he?). So, he was taking me somewhere, and I was following him blindly, as if I had known him for a long time. The coldness of this place made it hard for me to breathe. All I remember is that he was taking me somewhere when I collapsed due to the sudden change in atmosphere. I was not accustomed to the pure forest elements.

I thought I was going to die after this day because I had trusted someone this time. I don't usually trust, but this time my mistake was going to kill me. I should have written a secret letter to my parents.

When I woke up, I was in a room. It was a relief to see myself alive. I was in a room where everything was so ancient and placed properly. As soon as the stranger saw me wake up, he filled a cup with something he was boiling in a huge vessel, like he was doing some kind of witchcraft. He gave it to me, and though it smelled bad, he said it would warm me up. So, after thinking twice, I drank it. Surprisingly, it was a delicious soup-type thing that really warmed me from the inside. While taking slow sips, I started analyzing the room. It was a small house made from wood and a combination of bricks. The interesting thing was the spiritual objects collected from different regions of the world. There were many things I recognized, each from a particular region or continent. There were many things he had collected. Then my eyes fell upon the window. As I looked outside, I only saw white rays which don't even brighten up the room. He use lanterns to brighten his room. It must have been nighttime. I stood up and sat in front of him to start a conversion.

I asked the hermit/stranger/kidnapper/monk (I think I should call him the hermit; it doesn't sound good or bad), "Hey, Hermit, where are we? And why do you live here all alone? What is it about you that made me so relaxed when I saw you? And what are these things collected here? Is there any meaning in collecting these things where no one is here to view them? And why do you tend to live all by yourself? Don't you have family?"

The hermit smiled at me and told me to relax, as I was asking him many questions. He then watched over his vessel, added some herbs or some stuff, and started speaking. "I am a traveler who travels to different regions of the world to understand the world, its meaning, and its true purpose. I observe things, I have questions, and I try to find the answers for which I travel. I have found many answers, and some are still remaining, so I am here for those answers. The thing about questions is that you'll never get satisfied because there are infinite questions.

So Mr. Hermit, how are you going to find your answers here, where there is no human contact? And how can you travel freely? How do you arrange money for food? And how did you build this home? Did you make it alone, all by yourself?"

The hermit ignored all of my questions and started telling me his story. "Let an old traveler tell you a story, my boy."

CHAPTER SEVEN

The Beginning

It all starts in the year 1948 (29th May, 1948), the story of mine.

Let me begin my story before my birth, starting with my father. My father had two wives. Yes, he married two women. One legally and one with whom he ran away. **How selfish, isn't it?** He belonged to a very poor family living in a small village, where poverty was widespread before independence (1947). So, my father had to move in search of a city where he could find employment. He reached the city before I was born. My father placed both the other women in separate homes (or rather rooms, as there was no money to buy even a house). He arranged another room on rent for the first wife.

I was the first child born while they are seeking for the employment. And I am also the son of 2nd wife. I was born when they were traveling from one city to another. And it is different story which I don't know about. After a year when I was a year old. My family moved to a big city with bigger hopes. And my father gets a job as soon as we departed there.

After a year, the first wife was blessed with a son (as she had a hard time being a mother), and on the other hand, I was also blessed with a brother (Who is going to be an angry person).

My father stayed with us for a week and went there (to my stepmoms house) for a week, which my mother didn't like at all (no woman likes it). Also, my mother used to be a very angry person, which wasn't good at all. And just like our problems, three years passed. And my mother's aggressive nature had transferred to my little brother.

As everyone knows, life is so unpredictable and uncertain. It took a U-turn when we were not ready.

My father died after three years, and at that time, I was 8 years old. That marked the beginning of my life; I had to take responsibility for the whole household as the bread earner had died. So, I had to start earning, and I began working as a vessel cleaner in local shops, my first job. My mother started selling pickles and homemade foods. Days passed, and poverty, needs, and wants increased. It was hard to get anything at that time due to a lack of money. After one year, my mother became weaker and weaker; she was ill and suffering from leg-related problems. It was like her lower body wasn't much useful. She stopped working after a short period because moving became nearly impossible for her. Although she could walk a little, but it wasn't much. For making pickles, climbing and walking was needed. I thought she would stop, but after a period, she restarted making them. Regarding my father's profession, he used to be a priest. So, I tend to visit the temple where he was a priest. Sometimes I visited not to remember my dad's past, but to steal money.

(Why this Mr. Hermit is going and moving his story so fast?...... Let me just hear him first.)

One day, while observing how people gave money to the stone—a stone that didn't need any money or financial support—I took a magnet, tied it to a rope, and lowered it into the money collection box. When I pulled the rope back, it was stuck with coins. Coins (metal forms of money) were highly used at that time. I felt happy doing such things because I was going to keep that money for myself. In those days, many people served food in temples with a secret blessing inside the food—a coin. So, I waited for the server to come, the server who only came once a week with limited food pieces. These coins didn't make much difference as there was only one coin placed inside the food. Obtaining secret money had no risk of getting caught. The risk of being caught was in stealing money from the collection box placed in every temple, where people could give money without being judged by others. If

I got caught, they would surely beat me harshly instead of calling the police because no one wanted to involve the police due to the lengthy process. I also had a family waiting for me, depending on me. So, I couldn't take any step because my brother wasn't working, and my mother was unable to work. Thus, I stopped stealing after some time, as I did it during my free time, either in the noon or at night.

Four years passed like this; I changed jobs, from low income to high income and in those duration I became a half-graduate person, which was a good thing at that time. So, I was getting paid more. There wasn't much awareness of studying at that time, so I dropped out and started working full-time. I worked for someone else in the morning and somewhere else till 5 in the evening. In the meantime, I made many friends.

Believe me, DAVE, friends are really important in our lives. They are especially important for someone like me, where no one knows me or my family. And Friends will last long and they make everything worth it if you choose them wisely. They have the power to change you into a whole other level. They can support you, but they can also break you. I have had many experiences with good and bad people, but there is always one friend who stays forever, and fortunately, I had that one. That friend of mine has been with me since childhood; it's like we grew up together as neighbors. In life, if you get even one good friend, it would be worth it to have only one. And do you know **what the most beautiful thing in this world?**

As the hermit asked me the perceptional question, every answer can be right. I replied in only one word, which I wasn't sure about: "Nature?" But he smiled back at me and said, **"Everything is beautiful when it turns into moments."**

I believe **Moments** are the most beautiful thing in this world. Moments we make with others, moments of laughter, smiles, bonds, proud moments, fear, silent days, lonely times, late nights, or early awakenings. Those are the moments we always remember until our death. And they should be good ones to remember because we are here to fulfill our karma. And karma is a very beautiful thing and also a cursed spell. It is up to you. Let me explain to you what karma means to me.

(Everything is straight and correct, but how does Mr. Hermit knows my name. As he said DAVE in between the conversion?)

CHAPTER EIGHT

Echo of Destiny

DAVE as I just moved fast while telling, let me slow down now. I want to teach you whatever knowledge I have so I was excited and started speaking fast. And I realize that I cannot make you understand everything quickly. So I will slow down my story.

******

Let me begin DAVE. Just listen....And **wait for the end.**

In the vast expanse of the universe, where mysteries abound and cosmic forces shape the destinies of all beings, karma stands as a profound enigma to the human species, intricately weaving the threads of fate with the tapestry of existence. Yet, our comprehension of this cosmic law remains but a small stone of its boundless complexity, drawn from the whispers of ancient texts and the echoes of spiritual teachings.

Let me give you some summary.

For our protagonist, let's take example of - Ved. Karma is not merely a philosophical concept **but a tangible force that shapes our life's journey.** As he navigates the labyrinth of existence, Ved finds himself entangled in the intricate web of cause and effect, where every action reverberates across the vast expanse of time and space. In the heart of his being, Ved carries the weight of his deeds, both past and present, as he grapples with the consequences of his actions. Like a traveler wandering through the corridors of his soul, he seeks to unravel the mysteries of karma, to understand the forces that govern his destiny.

With each step he takes, Ved is confronted with the complexities of his own nature, **the interplay of light and shadow within his soul.** He witnesses the ripple effects of his deeds, the way they shape his relationships, his circumstances, and his very being of existence. At times, Ved finds himself ensnared in the web of his own making, grappling with the consequences of his actions. He experiences moments of joy and sorrow, triumph and defeat, as he navigates the ever-shifting currents of karma.

But amidst the tumult of life's journey, Ved discovers a profound truth: **the power of intention.** He realizes that true karma lies not in the actions themselves but in the purity of the heart from which they word/spring forth. And so, he strives to cultivate compassion, kindness, and selflessness in all that he does, knowing that these are the true currencies/ value of the soul.

As Ved delves deeper into the mysteries of karma, **he begins to see the interconnectedness of all things, the way each action echoes across the vast expanse of existence.** And in this realization, he finds a sense of purpose, a guiding light that illuminates his path through the cosmic dance of cause and effect.

So, as Ved continues his journey through the ever-unfolding tapestry of life, he does so with a sense of reverence and awe for the intricate workings of karma, knowing that every step he takes **shapes the course of his destiny and the destiny of all beings.**

CHAPTER NINE

Bonds of Adolescene

I really have encounter many people during my life's journey and many of them became a part of my life and memory.

Friends taught me many things during my life journey and many lessons I have learnt from them in both direct and indirect ways. In our ordinary life, there are **MANY WHO STAYS AND MANY WHO LEAVES.** Those who stays; give them the best reason to stay with us forever and be true to the true ones who helps us in completing our duties and who had help us in our even smallest aspect from becoming something to being something.

I was hitting teenage hood. Teenage is an age group where you become angry, passionate, wild and smart. I have also tried out many things (as during teenage days we urge to try different things), which we wasn't allowed to try out. As I am from India and also Brahmin (Holy ancient caste) it's not good to eat non vegetarian food, as per my family's customs and ancient scripture. (But I should call myself hybrid as my mother was from different caste). And by my foolishness and by the support of my friends I started eating non vegetarian food every weekend. And as a teenage our blood is getting warmed and full of passion with anger. We started playing many a different things and sports. Not professionally for sure because we have not a single penny for coaching fees andpurchasingequipment. So we can purchase anything which is already used by other and use it on our own by making it something useful. I had learned swimming in a lake; instead of learning it on swimming pool. Lake which used to be a little far from our home. We jumped from the heighted slope and fall down direct on the lake; sometime I also had felt the direct flat smash at the beginning (which was so painful). **In our life WE used to be our coach and LIFE used to be our teacher**. And life/nature makes no excuse while teaching us things, it has its own way of teaching. So I believe that we must go with the natures flow, as we have no money and had many responsibility from childhood, yet we survived each and every day by learning little by little, we also feared of many things, but we have only reached towards the teenage part.

(When I was hearing HERIT talking, I see that glimpse of memories was passing through his eyes. Mr. Hermit is saying everything fast like we don't have much time. So I will wait for him to finish.)

Ending might be different than what we expect.

At the period of teenage, life became more depressing, everything in life just doesn't make any sense. And my hormones started working on its own dangerous way. I just had more mood swings than I used to have before. I can be romantic person and at the same time I am angry, dead, smart, and philosophical person. Nothing makes sense in this world in this age period. I stopped believing in the reality. I felt loneliness even when I was surrounded by everyone. And by that scene I remember I had written some lines based on my life at that time.

MOON IS MY FRIEND.
DAY BECOMES MY NIGHTMARE.
RAIN IS MY COMFORT.
LIFE IS A HELL.
SLEEP IS A HEAVEN.
DEATH IS A DREAM
HAPPINESS IS AN ILLUSION.
EMPTINESS IS MY REALITY.

CHAPTER TEN

Navigiting Adulthood

Teenage days are often the most depressing. When someone you love doesn't prioritize you as they once did, it can be devastating and more of...**Pain.** Feeling of left alone with no one with you and seeing your loved with else. In our teenage years, we often feel misunderstood and opposed, a sentiment rooted in childhood experiences. For instance, being the only child until my sibling arrives can lead to feelings of neglect when parental attention shifts to the newborn, despite being a misconception. Witnessing a mother dote on a new baby instead of spending time with you can evoke jealousy and sadness, emotions that intensify during adolescence (And I was really feeling like a slave, who just works without getting love and affection). However, while crying in front of anyone may seem to weaken morale to me (as per male), it actually fosters emotional strength during adolescence.

Teenagers often feel incapable of expressing their emotions openly. This stoicism can be both a shield against the world and a vulnerability within the family dynamic. Despite feeling destined for solitude, familial obligations necessitate survival, especially when one becomes financially independent, as in my case it was with <u>my brother's schooling.</u> As I have to take care of his finances.

Alcohol became a regular indulgence in our teenage escapades (an exciting experience which was harmful), despite its adverse effects on health and judgment. I recall instances of stumbling home drunk, even spending nights outdoors due to intoxication. An Alcoholic person in home is a toxic trait for our culture. So,

Concealing ignorant behavior from my family was challenging.

<u>Human also want short term happiness for long term loss.</u>

At twenty, I secured a clerk position in a corporate firm (not by legal education certificate), providing financial stability to my family. However, life took an unexpected turn when my mother arranged my marriage at twenty-one, a common practice in India. Despite initial apprehension, the wedding brought joy and unity to our family. Adjusting to married life meant shouldering more responsibilities, including satisfying my wife's needs.

Arranged marriages, while traditional, often entail uncertainties regarding compatibility and personal preferences. Despite this, marriage brought newfound support and satisfaction, a contrast to the solitary struggles of adolescence.

Let me introduce to my best friend which I might have talked about in our previous conversion.

****

We both are friend since childhood. When my father and his family came here for the first time, they were our nearby neighbors who lived 3 street away. He was the first person I talked to after we shifted our home from different city. And we grew up like brother.

As I recall. Once he called to his house. It was the first time I went to his home. My mom used to visit his home but I haven't seen it particularly. We used to do all things together but I never visited his home before. And I was amazed by seeing that he was living in a graveyard. And boy oh boy, it has very scary & negative vibes that I never crave. And it was not first time going there, but after that day I frequently used to go there until he got married. We had lot of moment together. Our talks, our plays & our moments.

I had many friends, but he was the closest to me. I remember vividly those carefree days spent playing hockey in the graveyard, the thrill of the game interrupted abruptly one day when the ball hit my left hand with a brute force that sent shockwaves through my arm. And at my time summoning an ambulance seemed worlds away from our reality. In our minds, only true emergencies warranted such measures, and a visit to a government hospital was perceived as a daunting ordeal. So mostly we manage scares by ourselves.

We are really good at medical. My friend fashioned a makeshift support for my injured hand, reminiscent of the braces provided by medical professionals for fractures. In those moments, we became our own healers, trusting in our instincts and resilience. Seeking medical attention outside of dire circumstances was considered an extravagance. Medical emergency was reserved for the gravest of injuries. Thus, armed with resolve and makeshift remedies, we carried on, weathering the storm of minor cracks and bruises with stoic determination.

We passed our time, relentless, carelessly and unforgiving, marked our journey through adolescence. We bore witness to the hard and fast laws and principles that govern its flow, grappling with the enigma of its passage. Time, with its own ways, remained a capturing concept of <u>forever & beyond.</u>

Even though we tried hard to figure out its secrets,
Time kept its mysteries just beyond our grasp,
Reminding us of our limits as humans.

As we navigated the unpredictable currents of life, we grappled with the uncertainty of the future. The unfolding of events seemed predetermined, as if inscribed in the very fabric of our existence. Yet, amidst the chaos and uncertainty, one constant remained – the bond of friendship that transcended the trials and tribulations of youth.

Looking back now, with the wisdom of hindsight, I can't help but marvel at the resilience of youth. In the face of adversity, we stood tall, unyielding in our resolve to overcome whatever obstacles life threw in our way. And though the scars of those tumultuous years may still linger, **they serve as a testament to the strength of the human spirit, a reminder that even in our darkest moments, there is always hope.**

As I remember, I started doing consumption of Alcohol when I was at the age of 19. And that thing isn't really good for health. Sometime in between the way to home I used to fall down and sleeps wherever I want (sounds funny I know). There was even a night when I have to fall asleep on the graveyard the whole night (maybe alone or with...)

LOL! HERMIT.

Sorry I just cannot hold my laugh. But my imagination makes it hilarious.

No worries. The hardest part is to hide your stink and behavior at your home when you had consumed alcohol. But I do it very smoothly or (maybe my mom just tolerate my behavior because she cannot do anything without my father). Days passing quickly as I was into a good job and they have even promoted me in a short amount of time.

At the age of 21 I got married. And even my brother is hitting teenage at that time so he is also earning a little at that time, but as compare to me he skipped graduation. At my marriage day everyone in our family are gathered and we are very happy seeing them all. Everything looks so perfect at that time. And after a month, my best friend also got married. Things look pretty after marriage. Because you start experiencing things which you have always craved for. You get support from your partner and felt relaxed and satisfied from your partner.

LOVE IS A BOTTEMLESS FEELING.

But the problem with the arrange marriage is that. You don't know to whom you have married, her choice, her likings-disliking etc. And after my marriage as I have to take responsibility of my wife. So I started earning more. And tried to fulfill her needs.

And always remember DAVE:

YOU DO NOT GET WHAT YOU WANT,

YOU GET WHAT YOU DESERVE.

Dynamics

After 1 year of my marriage. At the age of 22 I became a father and I was blessed with a girl. I was so happy because for father his girls are like princess to him. Things got pretty awesome for some period when a lucky charm born. With my financial support I helped my brother to get a good job and he also got married after 2 years.

And as I skip 3 more years. I have 2 girls and a boy. My brother has 1 girl and 2 boy. Our family just expanded into a greater sum. And we bought a big house for our family.

And things started getting ugly.

Remember the first wife (my stepmom), I have told you in the beginning of my story? She came to me once and asking for my shelter. She wants to stay with us because she was all alone. She had a son, but due to some reason she lost him. And she wants to live my family as she count herself related to us. By seeing her my mother didn't respond so I let her live. She was a good lady. BUT...

Can you just imagine, two wives of same person in one house? Where there are 6 children. My god my home. So after my decision my mother never talk with me as much as she used to before. She lived in her room all alone. And my stepmom stays with my family.

So basically my home consists of 3 room, the upper floor was reserved by my bother and family. Down part has an entrance room which was reserved only by my mother. And the inner portion was reserved by my family. And when in your house you have four totally different background people. Which was my wife, my brother's wife, my mom and my stepmom. So it is obvious that their mindset is going to be totally different. And when you live in a joint family with this much people, it increases the chances of argument up to 110%. And with my brother attitude of speaking (which was worst). He always used to speak bad words in front of everyone. He was like a rowdy person of our house. And no doubt there should be one person in a house who is rowdy, when someone lays a finger on our family. But he also started showing even in our family. Which is not tolerable.

As I was thinking about my brother's bad behavior, I realized that all of my friends had bad temper. I used to roam with all powered up style. For once someone just came at my house and started arguing because of some kind of reason. And as soon as my friends know about this they don't even want to know who was in fault, they immediately kicked their bike and reached at that particular person's home. And warned him not to lay a finger on my family.There were many days like this, when we all involves in fight. We never let anyone leaves in peace. And it was like, one day a boy was passing through me and my brother. And my brother won't let that boy pass the road until he did 10 full squat. (Ragging)

And I think my support made him like this today. I was also of bad temper, but I play more of mind games.

Family crises are increasing a lot, there were even days when I have slapped my wife due to chaos. Love was fading, everyone was showing their true color. My biological mother don't talk with my family much because I let my so called stepmom live with us. So kids doesn't felt the joy of grandmother. My mother don't let my kids get near to him, and all of his money she used to give to my brother. My brother family also don't talk much because of arising arguments of daily. This all things got so depressed, because you cannot support anyone, because if you take side of one the other one gets hurt and vice versa. You just cannot do a thing, **cannot say truth, and can't say a lie.**

Sometime, Life become such a drag.

After all the crises it was natural for a being to get depressed and tired. Whenever I felt like this, I went outside to roam. Sometimes

I even used to drink. Sometimes I go outside and watch a movie. But the good thing about me is that, I never even tried and even thought of suicide. That was just far from my mind. Because I do believe in supremacy who always helps the one in need. I had done mistakes in my life. **But I always believe that a mysterious power is always watching me/us. Trying to connect with us. Trying to teach us. That power is beyond my/our understanding, and I believed in that power.** And we humans also possess power of choice. In life, we do many things which are not supposed to be done. Many mistakes, many lessons many achievements & many failures. But, we aren't supposed to stop at any cost. Because at last we know nothing. Even when we DIE in our dreams we wake up. As our brain doesn't create the scenario of afterlife **OR** maybe we don't want to know the scenario of afterlife. We humans always find our Self, stuck in the scenario which we have created by our own Self. At first I thought that there is always FATE that work as miracle in our life. But the thing is, fate DEPENDS ON US, whether we do it or not, it's up to us. Our fate is the consequence of our choices. We always have the choices of doing that particular task.

Many questions are UNANSWERED in this world. Many questions are yet to be discovered, but the thing in which I am sure about is:

THERE IS NO ONE LIKE YOU IN THIS PLANET,

NO ONE IS GOING TO DO THE THINGS WHICH YOU HAVE DONE.

NO ONE IS GOING THROUGH THE THINGS WHICH YOU HAVE GONE THROUGH.

YOU ARE THE ONLY ONE LIKE YOU.

<u>ONE TIME, ONE PLACE, ONE PLANET, ONE UNIVERSE, AND ONE CHOICE...</u>

CHAPTER TWELVE

The Wisdom of the Tree

Years are passing but one day, something changed. Once my wife's friend came to our house, which she usually used to come. And my brother just got tempered because of her frequent visiting. He asked that lady the reason of being here in a rude tone. And as my wife was also angry in nature. So the thing she said is "THIS HOUSE BELONG TO US". Whatever we do, you have nothing to do with it. When I heard that my wife had said something in opposite to my brother, I was pissed off (it does not matter that he is right or wrong) but I can't say anything to anyone. After what she said, my whole house was mad at her. She heard the worst word from our house, (including me at a point). Old time was really bad for women. Because no one respects them. People just see women as sex material and as a worker. Women usually aren't much involve in anything (because they are not allowed to). No one cares about what they want and what they want to do. At that time people have more children because of continuing legacy mind-set. Only boy can maintain the legacy, as girl gets married and their life is over at their own old house. The girl born was used to be a shame. And everyone scolds mother for giving birth to a girl child.

But by god's grace as next generation took place, all thought process changes and become different from the old one.

(I think that's why immortality is a curse).

The old thought process continuous if the old generation is immortal. Can you survive if there is immortality?

Humans are very disturbed creature. We humans have achieved the surviving purpose of life. But still we have concurred nothing yet. We never have unleash our true potential. Nor in the terms of mind nor in the term of physically form.... DAVE..

(Let's continue the story).

As I was saying, my brother was of angry nature, and angry people have EGO always by their side. So he decided to own a new house. So after one year. He really owns a house of his own with of course my help in money. And that was a pretty good thing for US at last.

I REALISED THAT WHATEVER HAPPENS, HAPPENS FOR A REASON. NO MATTER HOW HARD THE WAY IT HAPPENED.

Do you know DAVE you are meant to be **YOU** from the beginning? Simple question and might be foolish, but there are many who like to be like other, where they have to be like them.

In my early adulthood (before my marriage), I was at work and I was roaming here and there as it was lunch time so there isn't going to be much human interaction as noon is the rest time in my surrounding. While I was roaming. I saw a flying paper. And in a glimpse I saw something written on it. So, I catch the paper and saw it clearly. And the thing which was written on the paper was something beyond my understanding. It was very simple to understand, but words were very much weird for me at that time. The thing which was written on the paper was:

I WAS A TREE, BORN IN THE YEAR 1872. AND AS AN IMMOVABLE LIVING CREATURE, I USED TO SEE THE CHANGES IN THE TIME DURING YEAR BY YEAR. I HAVE SEEN THE DRASTIC CHANGES IN EVERYTHING. HUMANS ARE THE DUMBEST CREATURE I HAVE EVER SEEN IN MY WHOLE LIFE. DON'T KNOW WHY THEY CALL THEMSELVES THE SMARTEST CREATURE ON THE PLANET. AND THINK ALL SPECIES ON THIS EARTH CALL THEMSELVES SMART LIKE HUMANS DO. BUT THE THING ABOUT HUMAN IS VERY DIFFERENT, THEY DON'T HAVE CLAWS, FANGS, WEIGHT, HEIGHT, SHARP EARS, NIGHT VISION ETC. ALL THEY HAVE IS BRAIN. I AM TELLING

THIS BECAUSE, THEY DISCOVER EVERYTHING AND TRANSFORM IT CONVERT THAT DISCOVERY TO SATISFY THEIR NEEDS OR TO ACHIEVE THEIR SELFISH GOAL. BUT THE THING WEIRD ABOUT HUMAN IS, THEY CAN DO ANYTHING FOR THEIR WANT. HUMANS ARE ENEMIES FOR EVERY CREATURE EVEN FOR THEMSELVES.

AND I KNOW ALL ANIMALS DO THE SAME. THEY GUARD THEIR SHELTER, AND FIGHT FOR THEIR SURVIVAL. BUT HUMANS DO FOR THEIR BETTER LIFE STYLE. THEY CAN ACHIEVE ALL THEY WANT, BUT ON ANOTHER HAND THEY ARE FOOLS. THEY DO WHAT THEY WANT TO DO BY MAKING THEIR FUTURE IN DANGER. HUMAN THROWS NECULAR BOMBS ON OTHER HUMAN BEING TO PROTECT THEIR LOVED HUMAN BEING. THEY POLLUTED EVERY POSSIBLE THING. LIKE FOR EXAMPLE, THEY CUTTED DOWN TREES FOR MAKING PAPER, AND THEY GAVE TITLE OF "SAVE TREES" ON THE BACKSIDE OF THE BOOKS.

IN THE ANCIENT TIME IT WAS GOOD. LIKE THEY NEED IT, AND ALL ANIMALS DO SELFISH WORK TO SATISFY THEIR NEED. AS ANIMALS ALSO EAT MY GIVEN FOOD, AND MAKE SHELTER. BUT AS HUMANS GROW IN TERMS OF TECHNOLOGY. MOST OF THE WORK IS DONE IN SOME SCREEN. AS FOR COLLEGE AND SCHOOL STUDENTS. THEY LET THEM WRITE TILL THEY GRADUATE. AND THEY DO JOB IN THAT SCREEN. SO WHY WASTING SO MUCH PAPER? WHILE YOU CAN MAKE A GOOD SCREEN WHICH DON'T DO ANY HARM TO HUMANS AND ENVIRONMENT.

I WAS BORN, THEN I WAS CUTTED DOWN AND MY WOODS WERE SENT TO A FACTORY, IN WHICH I WAS CONVERTED INTO PAPER. AFTER THEN KIDS USED ME AND THEN I WAS THROWN AWAY AND NOW I AM FLYING SOMEWHERE WHERE I WAS USED TO BE DESTINED, AND SOMEONE MIGHT BE READING NOW.

I didn't understand a thing, and I still didn't understand that it was written by a human or someone unidentified (of course it was written by human) If that was written by any human. I salute to his words. He spoke the feeling of that tree. So connecting, touchy and understandably. But the thing which I was wondering is; why it came to my hand? A person who never reads, Read a paper which was flying out of nowhere. Sometimes I thought it was destined to be read by me.

And about destiny:

DESTINY is a very believing and unbelieving thing.
Destiny is the red thread weaving through the fabric of our lives, connecting past, present, and future in a timeless journey of purpose and meaning.

CHAPTER THIRTEEN

Ethics Unveiled

Destiny is a very illogical idea about how things is going to happen. For example: I am a right handed person, with CANCER as my astrological sign, with 3 mole in my body and brownish hair. Features which we are seeing in our body, I do believe it is not as natural as it seems. I believe Destiny works on all factor if my perspective is represented. Your all births are related to you, and as our soul is immortal and cannot die. Soul only changes the body. So if you are thinking this body belongs to you. You are definitely wrong. **You belong to nothing.** The world is more than what you sees in this world. The infinite equations is not a piece of cake. No creature in this universe can solve it out. And if we think we are close to the equation, it simply mean that THEY want us to play with them. THEY want us to believe in something. THEY let us understand us. And our destiny's role is played by an **outer force** which work as the mediator between this universes or maybe between all parallel universes. The way you write, way you talk and all things are just based on two factor CHOICE & DESTINY.

DESTINY can be changed by just using two different word at any situation and that two words are **YES & NO.** Your choices makes your destiny, so don't act dumb in future. And don't wait for destiny's activation while just doing nothing. We just have to do our ethics, it will activate on its own. Destiny has their spirits that protect it. And in this whole. Wherever there is light there is also darkness to be seen. In which every form you choose to see the perspective, there will be always a bad side of it, to see what is good and what is bad can only known by your perspective, because our background decides what is good and what us bad. **But the thing about perspective distinguishing is not always the accurate one.** Because, for the herbivorous animals the carnivorous animals are always be seen as the darkness (because they hunt them), but the truth is seen by others are different. For carnivorous animals it's their basic requirement.

Light needs darkness to be evaluated. Both need each other to be balanced.

Like bad spirits, I recall one of my incident. I was going home with my friend. We used to do each and everything (mostly) together. We are friends, since our childhood time. And while we were going towards home in bicycle. I remember clearly it was night and a lonely road. And we were carrying meat which attracts bad spirits. And while we are crossing the path we were pushed from our bike. And everything which we were carrying destroyed down (Destroys in the term for cannot be used again). That was the first time I have experience that type of thing. **I believe good and bad spirits are around us whether we believe it or not.**

On the contrary, as moonlight need sunlight. Because moonlight is actually sunlight that shines on the moon and reflects back. So I believe bad and evil power is just like moon, which needs good and pure spirit to work.

And DAVE you know which power is the powerful between EVIL & PURE?

MR HERMIT, I believe it's the pureness who surpass. Because unlike moon bounces back the rays of sun. So obviously sun has the high power.

No my son. I just have explained you by taking the example of sun and moon. While the pureness and evilness possess same abilities. Both have their own unique power. Both are similar, but their deed is only different.

I believe that, nor are the purest true powerful or the evilness. There comes **the third form**. Their **FUSION** is the most powerful one. There are the pure monster, which make the bad one - bad and make the good one - good. They like being in both the side, they work for both, they kill for both. And at last, they are nowhere to be seen.

The silent one are the most dangerous one, because no one knows what they are about do. They pretend to do everything while they don't have a single percent of interest in anything. They know what to do to make their surrounding chaotic. They know how to handle the situation according to the scenario. While the pure sees optimism in everything and evil see pessimism. But this fusion is a lot worst. They know how to do the thing to mess it up. I feared them the most because they leave the situation like it was nothing.

And we all aren't the bad people or good, we are just doing things which characterizes us. But sometimes we do something which we usually don't do. Sometimes we thinks that what we just did and why we took such action. At that moment you should understand that the fusions are behind it who planed everything and acts according. Those type of personality used to socializes while they disguise of human kind. They know how to control their emotions. I feared them the most DAVE. They smile in front of everyone while they have no interest in what so ever. Their eyes always seems different. They make lots of friends, and it was really easy for them to highlight themselves. But at last they don't crave for any friendship.

FUSION type of characteristic were seen since the human existence. GODS way of doing thing were different and DEVILS way of doing things are different. But fusion make their mindset opposite from each other and make the different partly negative in nature.

NO ONE AROUND US EITHER GOOD OR BAD, IT IS JUST OUR OWN PERSEPCTIVE AND HEARING FUSIONS PERSEPCTIVE.

CHAPTER FOURTEEN

Business Blues

I always believed that one job was never going to do a right thing. As I have mentioned before I was also doing side work in a business organization simultaneously while doing job. Since the day the Business was started I was there in that field. And the owner of that shop was kind of good, rude and smart. I used to be a sales person and maker. I was the all-rounder person, because in business you have to do all the things. The shop was not so huge and product was just a NEW thing for the whole region. It was kind of an awesome experience, and the work was so delicate that any mistake can burn your whole wrist and palm?

Situation was hard to handle sometime. When you are given with the responsibilities of the family and you don't even know about the functioning of the world & earning methods. Even in business I was given much less salary. And the work was more during that time, because as it was a newly product, people was eagerly waiting to taste it and we have to introduce it to the market. And in a slip of few duration, employee count also increased. But I was the most trust worthy according to the CEO of that small business. It was because they knew me since the beginning of the business. And I also have my contribution in increasing the sale of the business, because in our developing city, there was no three wheel cycle at that time. And I was the one who bicycled it to all the corners of the city to sell the product and to deliver the product.

Earning was all the main purpose of our life, I still knew that for earning, we pick the good flowers in the early morning before some vender cut them off and sell. We used to pluck them first (me and my friend) and then sell it to different venders. And we also do it for fruits and vegetable, we take some for home and rest sell it to the venders. We have to climb the different trees, where I encounter a snake, which looks venomous, and as I feared it the snake. I threw it by holding its tail. And I have did it fast before snake bit me. Me and my friend used to do this type of things when we have our day off. But after I joined the business I haven't had any day off.

Owner wasn't used to be so nice at our time. They used to exploit a lot. All they thinks about selling their damn product. The authority never even let any employee eat or taste the product. So the employees (including me) used to eat a handful of the food product when owner moves and goes out for some work. And as we are doing a food business, it was basic nature of human to eat a little while working. And owner should let the have some.

Relation between my family and owner's family began to build. Which is kind of weird, but yeah you cannot change the natures flow. And natures flow means the thing which is going to be happened is going to happen anyhow. So the relation was build, because I had served 2 years and still into it, and as I recall even the owner's children knows me. He has 2 boy and a girl. And as I was the oldest one in the shop as a worker, I had done many personal things for my owner and as I was about to retire from my job in 5 years and still I am 30 years in age. And the good thing is that I was going to be pensioned after I retires, so early retirement was kind of beneficial for me. Because I can even get to do more time in any other work and can generate more income.

Wait, wait, and wait. Mr. Hermit. I am sleepy now, now the rest of the story tomorrow. You have said a lot.

Tomorrow there isn't going to be continuation of story, because now it has been 6 days you are here and I do have to find some food for you, so tomorrow we'll go into the woods to pick some food for you, you need it more because I can survive without with for long days.

I asked hermit while yawning. How can someone even survive without food, are you even a human? And after asking the question I just slept. I think he do told me something at that time, because I heard the whispering, but I was not able to hear anything because I was too tired, tired doing nothing all for 6 days. And I think the cold temperature just made me more sleepy type person.

CHAPTER FIFTEEN

Journey to nowhere

Next morning. It was little lazy for me to wake up that early and I wasn't even expecting to wake up that early. But I woke up, because Mr. Hermit threw a cup of cold water on my face. And that was so rude of him. But I cannot even be angry at him, because his chakra level always calms me. I am no match for him in anything. He was so strong, calm & active person. We are no one in his comparison. But the thing weird about Mr. Hermit house is that there is no watch or calendar so that can shows the time and date. He once told me about how he sees time while looking the nature. Mr. Hermit, knows about time while watching the sun, day while watching the moon and month while watching the stars position. I have heard about such things but I have never seen it. For the first time I was seeing it physically. I usually don't care about the time reading right now, as I don't know how to see the time while looking at the star moon and natural things. I really don't know what time it was. But the time was before the sun. It is maybe 4AM in the morning. And Mr. Hermit gave me some clothes which helped me being warm, and he was as usual like always. Wearing thin clothes which he was wearing at the first time when we crossed our path.

We went off the house, at that moment I knew I am going to be so dead. The coldness was insane, like really insane. I just thought how he can tolerate such things.

I always found this place full of darkness, I haven't seen any sunlight near this place. There is no reach for sunlight. More I try to understand more I get weird thoughts about this place. It is like a place where everything is so unrealistic. Like how come a place like this haven't found by anyone yet. As long we started walking the more intense the jungle becomes. Like it is a jungle after all, at last it is a place where living a life is hard if you don't know how to survive, and don't have any survival skills. As we are walking towards somewhere, the fog is getting thicker and thicker, it was hard to see anything. At last it was like I was just following an image which is in front of me, and I am trying my best to be more nearer to Mr. Hermit as possible. This jungle is giving me more creepy vibes, it like I was in some kind of television show of any horror film. But it was worth being shoot here. For once, one must visit place like this, because the real thriller is only in places where there is less human reach. And has some mythology connect with it, some kind of back story, like I am sure this jungle also has its own, that's why there is a danger board near to the base point. I am much curious about many a things, like the pending story of Mr. Hermit, about this abandoned place which is here, out of nowhere. And I really do hope that everything gets over, because it's been many days since I had left my home. And I don't belong here.

As I followed Mr. Hermit for near about 3km, I was just stunned by what I saw. It really seemed like a HEAVEN. It is everything anyone wants to see. It is so aesthetic, that I couldn't believe that this type of place really do exists. And exists in my region and no one even knows about this so far. It is like, we have come from darkness to lightness, because here there is a little rays from sunlight that makes the place more beautiful. I would like to spend my whole generated income to visit places like this. Because this type of place is only worth seeing.

PLACES ARE NOT RARE, IT IS OWR NARROW PATH
WHICH HAVE'NT EXPERIENCED ANYTHING YET.

CHAPTER SIXTEEN

Essence of Love

When I used the word HEAVEN, Mr. Hermit asked me a question:

DAVE what is heaven?

HEAVEN is where all possible evens can occur. Our own needs and wants can be satisfied, no one is beggar. Everything is perfect there. Mind feels peaceful there. That's what HEAVEN is termed as in my perception.

Explain your thoughts about it Mr. Hermit.

HEAVEN is not a place to find,

HEAVEN IS YOU.

HEAVEN IS THE MOMENTS YOU FELT AND MADE. HEAVEN IS YOUR FANTASY.

HEAVEN IS YOUR THOUGHTS.

HEAVEN is also the people with whom you feel good, you feel comfortable, and you feel absence of time. HEAVEN is what you made it. Same goes with love. LOVE is what you believe in it. Based on your past, you termed the meaning of LOVE. But in reality LOVE is an unexpected process.

Let me try to explain the word LOVE, through a story.

DAVE, SUPREME ENERGY doesn't create everyone same. In our planet, there are many species and every species is different. The way of every creature is also different in terms of living. But we all are just performing the same thing for the same purpose, which is...

Survival, happiness and maybe satisfaction or freedom. What you want in your life? Every creature wants the same thing in different way. And as you know, there are so many different galaxies and so many universes. So, every universe has its own different power. There are infinite universes, and maybe there is one universe where communication is done only through vibration. In some universes, the purpose is to be the most powerful creature of the universe. In one universe, there is only killing to regenerate themselves to become something extraordinary. In one universe, there is only peace and loneliness that prevails. And there are infinite universes; the supreme energy releases thousands of universes while inhaling and exhaling. So we cannot even imagine the creation and destruction. In our universe, the books that are left out or written for us are only useful in this universe, and they only describe the creation of this universe. SO THERE MUST BE DIFFERENT FORMS OF WAY GOD HAS LEFT THE COMMUNICATION WAY IN EVER UNIVERSE AS PER THERE NEED AND WANT?

And in our universe we are here to find our purpose in which LOVE is the mediator to help us achieving that thing.

Mr. Hermit tell me more about LOVE.

Memorable hostel escapes

Love is something that is hard to explain. In reality, love is something that is hard to understand. Love has many forms and types. It is not a simple thing that can happen easily. Love requires time to develop and understand the needs and wants of every creature. Love is far greater than we think it is. It has the power to change a being. Love is the only great thing that has its own power. Whatever form love takes, it is powerful.

DAVE, love is so perceptual in every term. If you ask any human near you, you will find different answers. Even we both have our own different answers about love. That's why love has no boundaries. Love is described by someone only through their past and present scenarios. Someone who has a bad past and no good memories of childhood or has been rejected by their loved ones and is so broken that whenever they see others being loved, they show more and more hatred towards others. And that hatred causes ill feelings about love. And those who have felt love but still feel incomplete are about to find (or need) to start observing more about love. Their definition of love is different.

I suddenly remember a story DAVE, story about a boy. And after listening the story, I want your opinion about that boy.

There was a lovely kid around 14 years old, he was born in a very caring family and he was loved by everyone. And after he completed his 7th grade his father took a decision to send that boy in hostel.

On the first day he made a lot of friends due to his good personality. Everyone there enjoyed his company and liked him in the first impression. And after few months that kid started admiring his senior. He like his personality and his humor. And that senior was being liked by everyone in the hostel. Everyone admires him a lot and they all enjoy their days in hostel. That boy saw that senior like his brother. All the batch students used to do illegal thing which has lot of risk. And the thing about risk is that; when we succeed in doing some risky things, that joy is just unimaginable.

The hostel had a strict curfew: no one was allowed outside the campus after 9 PM. This rule was particularly crucial because most residents weren't young, and adherence to it was enforced. Moreover, possessing money was against hostel regulations. Situated outside the city, the hostel required students to travel far for basic necessities, given its remote location into to a jungle.

Given the responsibility of nurturing young minds, the principal had to enforce numerous rules. Venturing outside the campus was permitted only for essential purchases or temple visits. The hostel comprised five main rooms: three in the main building and one in the principal's apartment. There were two main faculty members, one of whom resided in the large apartment alongside students.

In the hostel, there were four rooms, with one room accommodating up to eight teenagers or children. Three rooms were on the first floor, while one was on the lower level. Among these, one room had children under 10 years old, the middle room served as a faculty room, and the last room accommodated older students.

Initially, the younger children occupied the lower-aged room, while older students resided in the last room. However, over time, the older students took over the last room, which boasted a balcony and access to the terrace. Bullying was rampant, to the extent that seniors would physically assault their peers without hesitation. Almost all faculty members, except for a few, resorted to corporal punishment. But that kids batch have a lot of fun, and as their batch is living with that one senior, they have all the benefits of watching movie in laptops. As mobile was not granted to any student at that time, it was fun doing it. And all the students kept their money hidden somewhere. And night when all lights are turned off. Higher aged students wake up like an owl. They all decide that who will go and buy food products for the group. And it was night time, they all must go in pair, so basically 2 students are being chosen. For this work, that two students are must be at their best physical shape because they have to climb all the way down. Because at night the main entrance was locked. Then they teens have to reach to the market which was maybe 2 km away. Not far. But the road was all lonely as it has less population out there.

The chosen ONE for this work. That one has to first jump off the wall which has height but there is also small store room connected to their room, and by the help of that room they easily get support and they have to jump off the gate all silently. And if a little bit of voice be made then the chief of the hostel wakes up. And they have to take the road where there is no lights, because there is mainly two ways of going towards the market, one way has the principle home and another one is from bush and underdeveloped abandoned place road, so they practically have to choose the dark road to not being caught.

The thing was thrilling until. Until our main character's (the sweet boy) turn comes. He and his friend who was just like him, fat and not flexible has to go to collect the things which were in list. They all laugh seeing those two taking different types of positions to reach down the main gate. Even they both are laughing at themselves. And as it was boys' hostel, there was no awkward moments. (*Then there was a batch of girls, which happened in future.*). And at the boys' hostel, best part was that: **Everyone has seen every colors of their roommate but still they form a unity in every single aspects.** Then after they bought cold drinks and food, they awake till night and used to enjoy a lot, they sometime scare those kids who used to have fear of ghosts. The senior let them watch movie in faculty's laptop. They used to watch many type of good, bad and horror movies. And after watching movie they talk about the spiritual things happened to them in the past, and those who are from village or rural area, shares their experience of paranormal activities they have heard of. As all rooms of hostel have dormitory beds, upper portioned child lays down like monkey and the lower portioned bed child, sleep like beer. That senior sleeps on the ground. While talking or watching movie, monkeys take their transformation and bear theirs. Which was so hilarious. They even burn the fire at the night time of winter at hostel. And they have to be very careful about all the things which I had mentioned you.

Once their faculty had captured them at night.

It was late night and they have just collected all the food items and faculty was not there, he was just a student so he sometimes come late. Everyone opened the food and they heard the footsteps of their faculty, they left all the food at its existing place, one turned the lights off and everyone reached to their beds and pulled their blanket to hide their body and face. At that night their senior also pretend to be in a deep sleep. But the turning off of light was being noticed by the faculty and the door was throbbed. And the sir turned on the lights and sees the food which was placed there. And as everyone was acting to be in a DEEP SLEEP. Sir told that whoever is awaken stand in front of me or I will punish every one right now. They all wakes up with an awkward and guilty smile on their faces. Then they were are surprised by what happened next.

That faculty joined them. And told them to fill the glass of cold drink and prepare the dish of snacks for him. Since after that there were many a days when that faculty orders the food and cold drinks. It like they have the best experiences of their days. Many types of things they have to suffer. Many things were heart breaking to see. But they have created many unforgettable moments. And DAVE I am telling you only one incident from that night era of the hostel life.

Happiness don't always last longs. They are only together for one competitive exam preparation at that hostel. After that all got separated. One year duration was just about to end. The boys who loved their senior; just disappeared before the exam month. He went outside for his master course. He didn't left his contact and was hard to find. He become god to ghost.

To the boy whom he admired the most suddenly became someone who didn't exist anywhere except in memories. Many experiences taught him, many lessons he imparted, and his perspectives shifted significantly. After that incident, he broke down and asked himself what had gone wrong. He learned one thing:

Nothing and no one in this world is forever. Forever is merely a concept existing within our emotions. Forever is only in memories, not in humans, for we are merely souls inhabiting changing bodies. However, when souls connect, it becomes eternal.

Many things are eternal, while many are not. **Many will stay, and many will leave.** Those who have a karmic bond with us, and those who are meant to form such bonds, will cross our paths. In this process, you will discover your true self because your surroundings shape who you are today. Your decisions and choices were made long ago, all connected to one energetic source, which every human, whether they believe it or not, acknowledges. If you believe a stone is significant to you and start considering it powerful, then it is. The point is that everything is interconnected, and our beliefs shape our reality. **YOU ARE THE SOURCE TO THE MEDIATOR. YOU ARE THE ENERGY.**

And by understanding that simple thing that boy started to learn and understand the simple rules of life. <u>The more you live outer in space the less you care about this world.</u> And his teaching is going to make who he going to be in future.

CHAPTER EIGHTEEN

Finding Strength

DAVE, I would like to mediate for a while and I would like YOU to go and search for our place and wait for me till I return. And take all the things which we have collected from the forest because it is going to take one week till I return, so I would like to take care of yourself in my absence.

Mr. Hermit. One week? How anyone can sits for one week? Don't you starve? And how come I find the way through the forest? I don't know the way Mr. Hermit.

DAVE the way is easy for reaching back, all you have to do is **just look back and start walking.** There is only one way to reach our place, but there is more possibility of you're getting lost in the forest, and if you do lost in the woods which I believe you will. Then try to survive for a week. I will catch up with you after a week.

Do you know what I think, Mr. Hermit? You have already planned everything: to take me with in the woods for give me a wild adventure. Am I right, Mr. Hermit?

Exactly, now if you will excuse me.

After saying me those words, he started climbing the mountain which was in slope. And I think that no humans except the ones who lives in the forest can perform this type of things. Seeing him climbing, all I can think about is, how I will survive in this damn forest all by myself? This is going to be a drag.

I started walking and if there is even the foot mark made by our walking steps then it would be easy to follow the path and reach there, but due to the fog and moist air it was vanished. This type of place in which I am walking looks beauty when you have proper guidance and a guide. But right now I am scared a lot. The more I walk the more I realize I am going to be in danger, but as per Mr. Hermit lessons, **we should not manifest the bad vibrations. And if we do, the possibility will raised up to its maximum level of happening.** So I was trying to be as calm as possible, and thinking of good scenarios, and here there is no difference between the night time and the day time because everything is just so damn dark here. So I just walk as slow as possible because I was saving my energy and observing the forest which seems little odd to me. I was observing at that time, as I was looking for a place to sleep and rest for a while, and in many stops I found some huge rocks which I know will protect me at some point, and as soon as I sees them I starts climbing them, and while climbing I do have many cuts and scratches. I was also bleeding but not to death, so it was basically fine.

"The first day stretched endlessly, a seemingly interminable stretch of solitude with nothing to grasp onto for support. It prompted a pondering on the human condition—how could one endure such isolation? Because if I talk about me, I always need a talking companion with me.

Once again, I found myself in an unfamiliar place, as Mr. Hermit had predicted perfectly of me getting lost. However, this time it was different. I was surrounded by the breathtaking beauty of nature and also with the frightened behavior of nature. With the stars shining overhead and the sky alive with a dazzling cosmic dance and with each moment I felt a bravery and beauty which was not suppressed by the loneliness. Despite the disorientation, there was a sense of contentment that washed over me, as if I had stumbled upon a long-forgotten secret of the universe.

As I walked through this unfamiliar terrain, the rhythm of my footsteps became a metaphor for my life's journey. **Each step was a reminder that we are all wanderers and travelers, moving forward on our paths unknown, driven by an insatiable curiosity to discover what lies ahead.** It was in these moments of aimless wandering that I began to uncover truths about myself and the world around me.

My trusty backpack, my constant companion on this odyssey, was a symbol of preparedness and resilience in the face of adversity. It contains - a bottle of water, a flint and steel for burning fires, a compass and a first-aid kit for medical emergencies - served as a tangible reminder of the essentials needed for survival which I am inexperienced of. But beyond that, it represented the importance of being ready for whatever life may throw our way, and the strength of character needed to overcome any obstacle. I was missing my parents. And I realized something:

We often think about our families and the choices we've made.

I often wonders if everything was planned out for us or if we're in control of our own futures. Mr. Hermit represents those mysterious things that affect us without knowing. Let me wonder the true brainstorming.

When we think about the lessons our parents teach us, we start to understand how they balance keeping us safe while also letting us make our own choices in life. When they give us permission to do things on our own, it's like they're secretly saying that, they believe in us. But there's more to family than just that - it's about the strong connections we share from all the experiences we've had together.

Understanding relationships is about more than just what we see on the surface. It's also about understanding our feelings and how we get along with others through our behavior. Forgiveness is hard sometimes, but it's about being able to forgive and understand others when things don't go as planned.

In life, we often wonder what keeps us going, especially when things are uncertain. Is it learning new things, making friends, or searching for something greater? Every step we take and every person we meet includes to the story of our lives, shaping who we are and what we believe in.

******

As the sun sets on another day of introspection, I am reminded of the impermanence of life and the beauty found in the fleeting moments. Perhaps, in embracing the unknown, we discover the true essence of our humanity—**a journey of self-discovery and connection, amidst the vast expanse of the universe."**

TO LOVE SOMEONE MEANS TO BE IN LOVE WITH THEM IN EVERY POSSIBLE WAY, IS TO CHOOSE THEM OVER AND OVER.

Because after my high school graduation, I learned many a things about the human nature. Currently I am studying in the university. I do have met many people from different region and many are foreigner. So living between different people from different culture helps us understand their different mentality. So I do have gained many an experiences by seeing them and how they act so differently in every scenarios. Because many are lot stronger in physique and many are so smarter, so it was easy to observe everyone, and what they have been going through and what they probably want to achieve in their short time duration. Because how rock hard the mind and physique are, but eyes. Eyes never lie, so I learned to understand more of someone's nature by observing their eyes, so I do believe that I do understand someone's nature easily. But I do still make mistakes making friends, because at the time of teenage the understanding lacks, because it is the only age of experiencing things. And no matter how smarter you are you will always be the foolish in understanding someone. And no matter how great your physique is, if you are mentally dumb and less energetic then you are still at zero.

(After 48 min of talking with myself I started reaching at some point, the point which I was unaware about)

I have discovered and learned many things which was usually hard to understand by normal humans. I started understanding the life of jungle which I find funny. And as I was living and travelling alone these days, I really found a mental peace + disturbance. But, my instinct were also developed, but due to lack of nutritious food, I do have lost some of my weight, which was bad. And overall I have to pass 4 more days until Mr. Hermit finds me. But usually I would like him to find me as soon as possible because I am getting weaker due to lack of nutritious food.

Days are passing and I am learning how to catch fish. As I was weak in terms of my physical condition, I cannot climb a tree nor can I do some hard work, so I grab a wood and sharpen it to make a spear to kill fish. And everything became so easy because of my bag pack. The days are passing and I really learnt many things while living in forest. How animal kingdom works and how they use instinct. And days are passing and Mr. Hermit is two days late to pick me up. I am surviving my official 9th day without help of Mr. Hermit.

When the days are converting into nightmare and moon is blossoming the forest at that time, I saw a shadow moving towards me, a dark part of a soulful creature who is none other than Mr. Hermit. I can sense the shadow by feeling his aura from a distant. Mr. Hermit does look like different personality as compared to previous days. He looks more confident and skinnier. I think he was so into his meditation that all his fat converted into energy and by controlling its breathing to be sit still for a particular time duration. And without food or water it is hard to do a single thing and he has not consume anything since the day we were separated. The more I see Mr. Hermit the more I want to know about him. Like how can someone be still walking with such low energy levels.

Mr. Hermit as you have said: I'll be lost. It happened to me, but thanks to be lost because I have had learnt many things about the forest and its way of surviving.

I was thinking how can someone even able to walk after starving for long period. Is he even a human?

Don't worry DAVE, I had just gone for 9 days which was my shortest duration. And for humans, maybe it's a good question.

God damn Mr. Hermit. Are you kidding? Because 9 days are lot for a human being to live without food.

DAVE that is the thing. **Whenever we experience something unusual, we termed that incident as supernatural or artificial. But the thing is WE DIDN'T EVEN TRY TO ACHIEVE THAT FOR ONCE.** And for me, practice made me do this. And it is not impossible to achieve. It takes time, yes it definitely take time to do anything. You cannot just do anything in one day.

YOU HAVE TO GIVE EVERYTHING TIME.

• 58 •

CHAPTER NINETEEN

Popcorn Path

We finally made it back to home on the 10th day, and I couldn't be happier. I was really tired and we ate a lot. As our way back to home, we had gathered a lots of vegetable and food. When we got home, we rested all day, and on the next day, we made a really delicious meal. It was so good that I couldn't stop eating. Tears filled my eyes because I was so grateful for the food. I had never felt so thankful before. It was a mixture of happiness and sadness. The basic concept is:

WE LOSE SOMETHING, AND AFTER LOSING IT WE KNOWS ITS VALUE. The food was ordinary, there is really nothing new in that meal, but as I had not eaten anything good in past those days, the food really felt like heaven to me. Same goes for everyone. We usually don't miss anyone. It's a basic human tendency to forget their loved ones at a particular period of time. The thing which let us value our loved ones, is the moment that we share with them.

So Mr. Hermit. Shall we continue our pending story?

Sure, so where were we at last DAVE?

You were going to retire in 5 years and you told me that you are also into the business work that even their children knows you.

Yeah, those children were really amazing children. They were really calm minded, full of knowledge and ambitious. After 5 years when I was retired from my government work. I became a full time employer at that shop.

And let me tell you that the work I was doing was related to food & snack. And that snack was POPCORN. So basically I was talking to you when there wasn't much of awareness about that product. And when the product is new, people become curious about knowing the product. Sales grows with few months. And we start selling our product to different states and it enhanced the selling of our product. Days were passing and we have done a huge progress. In the small shop the workers counter had gone on rampage after a year. Like there were 7 employees in a small shop. And my owner took the permission of having monopoly in that particular area, which was fabulous and cunningness.

In business many deviations, loss, and even quarrels are normal. But, the most important thing is mutual understanding between the staff members and upper level management. As it makes a huge impact on the managing process. And most likely thing about this business is that, many leaves and many joins throughout years. I was also once offered as an employee with high salary in many different places with the same work. But I have decided to only stick to that job for as long it exists. Because loyalty is and will be the most important factor in anything. Time never settles for same.

If your one arc is good then your another arc is supposed to be bad and that's what the flaws of life is, and you have to accept it. Times get hard. There was even the time when I was crying because I was so tired of everything. What was going to happen with me and what is happening with me was so unexpected, because as I was so poor that my wife has to sell homemade products for selling. I didn't even realize in which standard my children's were studying. I didn't even knows in which school and classes they are going or which course they were pursuing. All I know and want my son to be an independent person, and for girls to have a great husband. Because at that time, women were mostly housewife. And mostly they take care about the housing stuff. So I usually don't cares about their studying. But I know that my both girls was topper of their class. They were hardworking in compare to my son. My son had no good abilities. And as he is a boy he can do whatever he wants to do. Because in compare to girls, boys used to have more freedom at that time and even today. DAVE always remember that no matter what so ever happened in the past or what so ever is going on present and what so ever is going to happen in future.

ALWAYS REMEMBER THAT REGRETING
IS GOING TO REGRET MORE.

At the time of decision, your decision must be foolproof. Because regretting is a sip of poison which always kills your brain through process. **And regret shows that you have failed in completing a task which doesn't even matter.** Some regret of raising children in a bad way, some are regretting that they are unable to confess their love and some are regretting of their choices. So for this instance, I would like to give you advice that before doing anything you must give yourself some time to think about it. Because your life is partially based on your decision.

CHAPTER TWENTY

Path of Silence

DAVE this world is nothing but an illusion, but we have to do what we are supposed to do.

After skipping few years, my boss dropped a bombshell on me: he wanted me to take over his shop. At first, his words didn't quite sink in (obviously this type of thing never digests at first.). As I remember, once he said to sell this business to someone and at that point I respectfully said to give it to me instead of giving it to someone. And I said that you will not get disappointment. But as he explained further, it became clear—he was entrusting me with his cherished business while he was ventured abroad, even proposing to be his partner in the venture. It took a whole day for the weight of his decision to settle on my shoulders (and it was spinning on my mind). As a mere employee, I couldn't fathom why he'd hand over such a prosperous enterprise to me, by passing his own kin. I know I had asked for it. But it was a perplexing scenario, for typically, such inheritances are reserved for his close relatives. The mystery of why he chose me was never been sorted out and I even hesitated to ask. Nonetheless, his gesture elevated him to a godlike figure in my eyes because now I have something of my own. And when something good happens to any human. At that time only they go to their ENERGY in which they believe in. But for me I always pray to my energy. And I always believe in my supreme energy. That they are always watching over me and this happens (becoming the owner of the shop I was working in) because they knows what I have suffered through, **our supreme energy always watching us.**

But as I become the owner and when my boss left the country. I knew that it was going to be hard. Because as an employee the work load is always NOT going to be easy and also as an owner of the company, responsibility increases. Employees generally do the work which they were assigned to. But as an owner we have to do everything, and we have to think everything. And since beginning I knew that I am not going to be a worthy person as an Owner, because from the beginning of my life, I was given the task to fulfill my duties given by my owner. I never have thought of becoming the authority. And I knew that I cannot order or give any task to my employee, because all those years I was so into work that I never thought of ordering anyone, and literally I cannot order anyone like a boss (because an order fulfilling person I cannot be a CEO person overnight.)

And the good thing which happened was that, the shop was named for my son. It means I am not the owner of the shop my son was. So I was basically working under my son's shop, how amazing it was. And the thing was, he was more interested into business than jobs. And particular we were in that kind of region where people wants their business instead of doing jobs. So my son was born with a business mindset, but I want him to be in a good job, which was kind of mean to say. But I was that kind of person who wants my son to start a job and he did as per my command. I was bossy when it comes to my family and I wasn't bossy when I have to be (in business). Many problems started popping out. Because in business all factors starts occurring in many ways. And my older daughter's marriage was done before I become the owner of the shop. So it was so hard to make marriage possible as per mine low earning days. But it was all done happily. The thing about my family was, everyone was born weak since the birth, because of my wife ill genetics.

When I married to my wife, I knew she had a chronic illness that might affect her, but thankfully it didn't. Despite our family faced several challenges as all three of our children were fragile and struggled with various health issues, making them sensitive to climate changes and other factors like not gaining weight in spite of eating fatty food. Despite those difficulties, I had always cherished my family deeply, and one should always cherish no matter what kind of family they have. Everyone is born a Germ. Just polish is needed. Some don't understand the polishing and some will.

During my second daughter's wedding, disaster struck when my shop was targeted with malicious intent. Initially, I couldn't discern the reason behind the attack. It was later revealed that someone with ill intentions toward our business orchestrated it. I recognized the culprit, a politician, but felt powerless to confront them due to their influence and my own timidity, and obviously I cannot stand a chance as I have a family and I don't want my family to suffer. They want to close my shop. Because some powerful authority want to do something with that place or just want to remove my shop.

It was a difficult time, and my reluctance to confront the situation left me feeling like a coward. Nevertheless, my love for my family remained unwavering.

So, I appeal for the good location for my shop. And my boss who was my partner helped me at that time. WHEN YOUR EVERYTHING IS ON LINE AT THAT TIME IT IS ALWAYS DIFFICULT TO ACT, because I don't want to lose the shop after so much trauma I have faced. I was so afraid and kind of depressed at that time, because on one side my shop was gone and on the other side my second daughter's marriage was about to happen. So it was all difficult for me, and my son started doing job at a very small age, even though he was not even at his legal for going job. He was always weak in studies in compare to my daughters. He just want to earn money and with only one goal he started moving forward. And wasn't even supporting nor encouraging him for clarifying him, because as I was the main bread earner of the house and plus for bonus he was earning. I was disturbed. So I just let him do whatever he wants to do, which I shouldn't had. Despite my flaws, my son was always a good, dependable person of our family.

CHAPTER TWENTY-ONE

Beyond Illusion

DAVE really after being the owner, I do have earned a lot of money and I haven't seen that much of money in my entire life. And my boss, who recently relocated with his family, saw something in me - my loyalty. Loyalty, I believe, is earned. While money can afford materialistic possessions, it cannot buy emotions. To truly capture someone's heart, one must resonate with them on a deeper level. Money only fulfills needs not the soul.

After my modest success, my wife began to travel. In the past, she mainly journeyed for religious purposes, but now she explores far-off destinations with others, experiencing the beauty of the world. After few years I also started travelling, just fewer places, often accompanying my wife. And our travels increased after our son's marriage.

My wife was a hardworking woman with a tender heart, and traveling to such places often brought tears to my eyes. I never thought that a poor person like me would even travel to a nearby location. I never imagined that I would be able to travel so far and see so much of the world. Nature has its own beautiful places, many of which I had never dreamed of. I had never seen snowfall before, and when I did, it scared me. I was bewildered, wondering what was falling from the sky. It was kind of hilarious, I know.

As I traveled, I saw many places and learned about many different things. I began to understand how different people around the world live. I never thought I could ever see and live with people from different cultures. One thing was for sure: there are many people like me who have suffered, who have been through a lot, and who still act like nothing has happened in their lives. When I heard others' stories, I couldn't even feel my previous pains and sufferings in comparison.

Always remember, DAVE, that in this world, pain and suffering are constant & everywhere. Many people endure such immense suffering that it's hard to believe it could even happen to anyone. For example, there was this man who worked as a transporter, riding his bicycle to carry people from one place to another. He only got to see his family once every five years. (Unlike me, who grew up without a father.) His children had their dad around, but they still carried the same responsibilities as I did when I was young. And despite earning very little, the man remained hopeful, even though he faced doubts, pain, suffering, and grief. I could never have imagined a life like his. The more I traveled, the more I seemed to understand about life's complexities. Each new place and each new story added layers to my understanding of the world and the resilience of the human spirit.

THE MORE YOU KNOW ABOUT THE WORLDS THEORY, YOU WILL FIND NOTHING AT LAST.

DAVE the world is so much complicated to understand, one as the life goes by I learned one thing for sure, that there is some reason behind your birth.

AND BELIEVE ME DAVE,
"NATURE KNOWS HOW TO CREATE ITS FLOW".

And once I think that I had meet my supreme energy coincidently. The story goes like, I was in a trip with my wife and I was in a temple at night time. Night time because we reached to that particular place during night time. We had to hold because of the traffic occurred due to rock fall in the hilly area which is known to be a common thing. And I have seen something which I will never forget, one rock falls on the bus and the bus was destroyed. There were many passengers in that bus, around 20-30 and they all... I have never felt that experience before and I hope I never will. I was just thinking about their family member's expression when they are going to hear about their loss. And in the mountainous region it was normal for local people to watch that kind of scene. So we were late at that time to visit that huge temple which was situated on the top of mountain. We all stayed at a restaurant for one week due to the expectation of falling rocks. And after a week I was seeing the temple which is not a piece of cake for everyone to see throughout their whole life. As I recall that day, I was in the back line/last line because in the temple usually ladies were the prioritize creature. I have always seen ladies on the first line. And there was a lot of smoke, because of the incense. One guy was near me and started talking while asking me many questions like: where I am from and what was my business and occupation. And I was really not into his questions because who asks business questions in the temple? He was a person from our bus if I remember right. Meanwhile he was boring me and telling me the things which I have not even asked for; one person came from the direction we are facing and all the sudden the priest of the temple blow the conch shell, and DAVE that sound is enough to make everything positive in your surroundings. As I was standing, that guy coming from opposite direction crashed with me and we both fell down.

The person who had been asking me questions helped me getting up when he saw me on the ground. I asked if the other guy was okay, but they (he was not only one lifting me) ignored me and just lifted me up. When I looked around, I didn't see anyone else who had fallen. When I asked again, they all said they hadn't seen anyone crash into me. It seemed like they hadn't seen anyone coming towards me. And they thought that I was fell by myself. Since it was getting dark, it was not easier to see what had happened. I started to think that who the guy bumped into me was. Because at first, I thought he might be a thief trying to steal from me. But several people said they hadn't seen anyone coming my way, and nothing was missing from my pockets. I was surprised by what had happened and how the guy had vanished. I realized it might have been something supernatural, especially because India is known for spiritual things. People often feel something strange or special there. From that day on, I knew there's always a spiritual connection around us. And trust me, Dave, you're never alone. **There's a bond we all have to honor in this world.**

In the wake of the collision, I pondered the fragility of existence. Life's journey, like mine, is marked by unexpected encounters and unspoken connections. As I stood amidst the confusion of the thing happened to me, I contemplated the mysteries of human perception and the illusions it weaves. **Could it be that reality is a collages of shared experiences, woven by the threads of consciousness?** The fleeting nature of our interactions reminded me of the transient nature of existence itself. In the chaos, there lies a silent wisdom, urging us to embrace the unknown and acknowledge the interconnectedness of all things. From the depths of uncertainty arises a profound truth: we are not merely solitary beings navigating the cosmos but vessels of a universal consciousness, bound by an invisible thread of destiny. So, DAVE in moments of solitude, remember that you are never truly alone, for the echoes of our shared humanity resonate eternally.

And the more I think about that abstract presence, I always starts thinking about many stuff which make many a thing illogical and difficult for understand. Because we know that there is something around us, but at the same time there was nothing but an illusion. And DAVE as I told you earlier that we humans know nothing about this world. We don't even know that whether we exists or not. Many things tends to be illogical..

******

Now DAVE, we will talk tomorrow and let me have some sleep, because sleep is the most important factor of human life.

Mr. Hermit, I want to go out today. I mean go out all alone. And even I want some experience of forest as it will not be that difficult to survive for me now. So should I go Mr. Hermit?

Yes DAVE, if you have confidence, then give it a try, and I'll wait for 3 days until you comeback or will I have to find you again? Always remember DAVE, forest has its own life. And you still know nothing about it.

CHAPTER TWENTY-TWO

Thread of Life

I packed my bag, because bag pack is going to play a huge role, and I have to make sure that everything suits well and must be well arrange.

And there I go. I packed everything, and as I just opened the door, the pink air of the atmosphere kissed my body. And in reply my body shivered. But this time my body shivers because of the cold breeze. So I shut the door closed, because it was too cold out there and I really don't want to take such risk to go out alone, because three days is enough to be dead. And I don't want to die at this small age, after being kissed by the air (pink air). Without any further thoughts and hesitation I put my bag aside, and stated making my bed at that very moment. I'll go someday else but for now I'll just rest for the while, because as Mr. Hermit said: sleep is the most important factor in human's life. So I'll rather sleep than taking risk.

And when I see Mr. Hermit's face, there was a smile, so basically that mean only one thing. That he knew that I was going back and going to sleep. So now I would rather sleep instead of thinking more. Good night Mr. Hermit.

(Next morning)

Mr. Hermit you were on my dream last night.

And what I was saying to you DAVE? I forget.

(I know I don't have to think about Mr. Hermit's power, but how did he know that he was saying something in my dream?)

You are telling me about HOW people hurt us the most.

And in the story which I was listening in my Dream was normal. Nothing crazier happens in that story, but the moral is what I liked the most. There was a girl, who is shy and introvert in nature. She was smart and intelligent with a good sense of humor. She lived with her joint family. She lived a very decent and a healthy life from the beginning and she was smart enough to understand everything. She had her own theories and different understanding from others, she thinks the way no other used to thinks. Many people around her called her more mature enough at her age. She was 14 and she had knowledge of various things. Even she had taken lectures of students of his age and she also tries to help in understanding the astronomy to her grandparents, it means she was smarter to teach her grandparents about their most observing topic, and she told them the things which they have never heard or imagined of. She don't love anyone except his family members.

Life is ever-changing & nothing lasts forever. <u>From the stars in the sky to the moments we hold dear, everything is temporary.</u> This reminds us to appreciate each moment and find beauty in the flow of life.

She knows that, whom she loves the most is going to leave her one day, so she try her best to move to another place for studying as she knew she cannot tolerate the loss she is going to suffer in future. She was preparing herself to handle the worst scenarios. So she left her home at the age of 16. And shifted to hostel for studying. She always try to distract herself from her family by making new friends and by joining and participating in new activities But inside she knew that she was more damaged than before, she just miss her family a lot when she stuck in some kind of emotional sentiment. And there is saying that THE MORE YOU IGNORE SOMEONE, THE MORE THEY DRAWN TOWARDS YOU. To her, all the memories came near him. So at the age of 17 she knew that, what she was trying to do is not going to help her in future. As she understood that she was going to remember her family whether they are with her or not. So she started spending more time at home on every weekends and later after graduation she started her further studies in her hometown. She used sits with her grandparents and listens to them, try to understand them, their pain and suffering, their beliefs and stories from what kind of situation they have passed their days. She spends time seeing how her parents work in business with others, how his father works and how everyone interacts with him, how everyone sees him, and how they saw her because of my father's reputation. She saw the calm mind of her mother, how patiently she done everything in her life. What kind of struggle her mother was gone through and by listening her parents and grandparents stories. Their working lifestyle made her felt regretted for being not close to them much. At the age of 19, she lost her grandfather. At her grandfather funeral, she wasn't sad at all, no tear had flowed. At the age of 23 her grandmother died and at the age of 48 her father died and at the age of 55 her mother died and at the age of 65 her husband died.

But to that girl/women, no tears has been sawn at the time of funeral. Everybody thinks about how strong that person is, how she accepts the single fact that everyone is going to die, and with that thing in mind she has no regrets of losing her family because she knows that death is constant.

Everyone was right. She had never cried at funeral but she misses them every day, because memories is what they left which kills a person from inside. She wasn't prepared for anyone death no one is ever prepared because

It's truly painful when you have to part ways with someone unexpectedly. The bizarre of their departure can feel like a heavy blow, leaving you overwhelmed with grief and disbelief.

I believe she was already dead at the age of 14 because she understood the concept of losing someone.

This type of story was something I have seen in my dream, it is not some kind of great story but it has many lessons.

DAVE, whether the story was good or not. Always remember one thing.

No story is worthless

&

Every story has meaning.

In this vast universe, we're all connected in ways we may not fully understand. Each of us is like a unique thread woven into the fabric of existence. Our stories intertwine, shaping the grand tapestry of life. Even though we may feel alone at times but we're part of something much bigger. Our experiences, our joys, and our struggles are all part of the cosmic dance. So, embrace your uniqueness, knowing that you're an integral part of the universe's intricate design. And no story which you have seen is worthless. Whatever you are understanding and learning from life is an integral part of life.

CHAPTER TWENTY-THREE

Invicible Thread

Mr. Hermit, now resume your story.

As previously I had told you my accident with supreme energy without knowing them. That was scary with heart melting experience. DAVE the world is so mysterious place that we have no idea about our own capabilities. Some individuals reach their fullest potential, becoming elusive figures in the world. Their presence is elusive, hard to find. You can't seek them out; if you encounter them, it's because they allowed it. They seem to effortlessly navigate life, as if their actions flow through them, not from them. Sometimes, they find themselves acting without conscious intent, yet fully aware. Despite this, they may struggle to find purpose in their actions, feeling like mere observers in their own lives. Many cycles intertwine, but we're only attuned to a fraction of them.

DAVE as I mentioned I have travelled a lot, let me tell you a story about love. Love is the only thing humans are capable of doing, which is what I used to think according to what I have read and seen. But now-a-days it is hard to understand ourselves and the love language of our partner. No individuals spent time on themselves for knowing their likings and disliking's. And when human don't understand themselves, how will they understand their partner? Reality is always different when it comes to understanding someone's nature.

It is story of a girl who was a foreigner and due to his father occupation they have to visit places according. And when you are somewhere where everything looks so different, you felt an anxiety about everything which you are surrounded by. You feel so suffocated seeing different scenarios you never imagined of seeing. And once the girl had experience the village like place, she was always been shifted to the city or modern area, but it was her first time she had gone through a place which she was not expecting. But she had to resists and be adaptive for few years. The place is situated on the mountain.

(Is Mr. Hermit speaking about Lucy?) The girl is going to live her few years in the mountains. In the mountain region where she went to school, she met a boy who caught her eye. He was tall, smart, muscular, and had an air of mystery, like the vampires in movies. (He isn't talking about Lucy.) He was only focused on his studies and job. And rarely use social media. Despite everyone knowing where he lived and worked, he remained distant, speaking mainly about practical things. His reserved nature intrigued her, leaving her curious about what lay beneath the surface. The girl has made many friends, means mostly all are her friend in class, because it is said that mountain people are most likely to be of WELCOMING nature.

It's said that girls cannot resists mysterious identity, so she wants gather much information about that guy. And she finds out that every girl from her group have crush on him. He was destined there 2 years ago. He lives with his parents. His parents are working on some kind of analytical thing. And the guy used to work at a chemist shop nearby (for approximately 4 hour).

And apart from the classroom stories. That girl used to have a habit to write a diary about her questions and daily abnormal things. She had a very distinct point to write. No matter how extrovert a person is, but by the end of the day. Everyone needs silent and personal time. She used to climb a small hill where she can view the town and write whatever she thinks of. And very few used to come at that distinct place as it was little far from town. She used to write about everything and used to draw sketches of sceneries, she liked the place for its vibes. And after one month, while she was writing, she glares him coming towards the mountain and unaware of her presence. Her heart beats at the first glance as she had not expected him at that moment. He climbed and he then sits on the hang and from his leather bag took out a book which was bided in an olden style. There were no such crowd. Because it was not a famous place. And if you are living in a region with less population. You will find many empty. After a while of doing their work which they are into. They glare at each other coincidently. And as soon as the awkward moment was created for the girl, she switch her glare in an instant reaction. And as soon as the boy saw her, he started walking towards her. He gets closer and closer to the girl and he asked for her permission to sit with her. That girl was shocked and in a sudden beating of heart she said YES. While they were sitting boy asked to kill the silence: why are you sitting alone? Are you all right? The things which let them connect was the SILENT NATURE.

They both started talking and after feeling the bond and connection, it becomes their weekend pattern on that hill. They often meet each other in the beginning. And after a while they started meeting each other regularly during the sunset time, he went at that place because he likes to be alone and at that particular place he can think, speak and talk with himself (basically he can do whatever he want) and now he has a companion who wants the same thing like him. They talked about their pasts and found many things common. And when it came to experience, it's normal for kids whose parents moves a lot, to have similar stories. They chatted about different places they'd lived and she learned he'd spent most of his life in old-fashioned places rather than big cities because his father was a very famous monument architect. He knew a lot about ancient civilizations, about it's created, and spiritual stuff, which she found really interesting. On one day, they were late due to little rain. So they were waiting under a tree for rain to stop. And after few minutes of waiting, the clouds were moving and the sky was graced with a full moon and they both were mesmerized by looking at the moon while talking, its luminous presence illuminated their conversation. He spoke of the ancient tales that elaborates about the moon god and goddess, drawn from diverse civilizations. Among these stories, he shared a story which belief deeply rooted in love. In those stories, people represented moon as love itself. **They believed that if someone loved deeply and talks under the moon light, the moon would always remember them in spite of the relation.** According to one ancient text, the moon is described as the epitome of love itself. Legends whisper that those who embrace love unconditionally are ensnared by the moon's enchanting radiance, forever etching them into its celestial tapestry. With a soft intensity in his gaze, he whispered to her, "Every time the full moon graces the sky, let it be a reminder of our connection, bound by the timeless thread of friendship." They become close friend from that day forth, and obvious that when two opposite gender meets with each other, the bond is created automatically. But everyones priority changes according to the time and situation. Their parents also know about all this, even their parents also become great friends, and once in every weekend they arrange a get together. And none of the school mates know about them. Many ups and downs came into their life, but it is said that those who are meant to be truly yours, always finds a reason to stay. Or to leave. And if you open their wallets you will finds a picture of both, taken in a photo booth, because photo booth was the only way at that time when they used to clicked their memories, because the smartphones are not yet to be used and introduced to them. But life always takes twist unexpectedly and, you cannot decide who will stay and who will leave.

Boys' parents have a transfer within a month. And for that girl it was still one year left to change the place. And they made every possible memories they could possibly make. They both become the real friends. **And friendship always happens unexpectedly.**

****

(After 2 months)

Sometimes we are surrounded by everyone and being loved by everyone, but still we felt that hole in our heart, and hole which was made after he left her. And after someone leaves you, no deeper contact is going to be helpful when live interaction of that person is not there. She goes at their place on the hill daily and misses him a lot. She also has its friends but she always felt that voidness. **Time helps us forgetting people, but it never let them fade from moment and memories.** And at last we always a finds a way to survives without someone, because we have to. And the greatest thing is that when we really loved and cared for someone, they are always meant to leave us many time.

For that girl, whenever she felt a sense of oneness with someone, either she left them or they left her. This was how the lives of many goes by, and we mistakenly think that they like being alone all the time.

****

Years and years had passed, girl married someone else during the time of her job (who is love of her life), and she had one son and one daughter after 3 years of her marriage. She lived a life she want to be lived, a middle class women with a satisfying job and having a caring husband. Having children and to live a life as a mother. She was living a life working and in a disciplined manner. She does workout with her husband and they are both really fit during their adulthood. They did meditation. Helps their children in academics. And raise them how a children should be raise by parents.

<u>And with a blink of an eye</u>. After being a grandmother of two girls (those two granddaughters only had one year of the age difference.) And when her oldest granddaughter turned 22 years old, she lost her husband and her only first love. And death is roaming near her because of her old age, she was near 75 and was suffering from weakness due to the age. Shen she was sitting near the balcony of her house. There was no light in her room so she told her granddaughter to light the candle so she can see those pictures. Looking at the pictures of her marriage album, he finds out every memory of her past and started crying because she was enjoying the glimpse of time and suddenly she felt a hole. So he told her younger granddaughter who was sitting with her, to give her a packet which was in the cupboard (a secret and small space under

the cupboard). She gives key to her granddaughter and she open it and give a package which was wrapped there. Granddaughter then opened it and amazed to see about their before marriage photos and photos with her friends. She started watching all the photos which she was shuffling while watching. She also asked her grandmother: which picture holds what kind of memories. In response grandmother told: Those photos hold a lot of memories, like where they were and who they were with. Unfortunately, because the box was never opened after your father was born, many of the pictures are now blurry or damaged. It's sad to see the photos in such condition, but the memories they hold can still be cherished and shared. You could try to digitally restore the damaged photos or write down the stories behind them to preserve those memories for the future. She still remembers every face weather it is damaged or not, because that packed which stored this all picture were most important people of her life, not only the people with whom she had good experienced with her but also with which she had a bond. They all were the passenger of her life after that they have never talked because of the time lapse. But they had placed a huge role in her life. And at last while shuffling, there was a Polaroid picture, a picture she never thought of seeing again, at first she didn't understand that who is in the picture and when she had taken that image. She became sad all of sudden and she started a silent cry, and silent cry always comes through heart. She told her granddaughter the story of that GHOST from the picture. Which she had long forgotten but after remembering that incidents from that image she never wished to forget him again.

She was so happy seeing those images and all the sudden she asked her daughter that when is the full moon again. Her daughter told her that it is today.

And while laughing, she left her soul from his body. She died with a blush, a tear, a smile and a laugh. She had lived every aspect of living life and died satisfied.......

AND DAVE SOMEONE HAD TOLD ME THAT NO MATTER HOW HARD A LIFE IS. BUT WHEN IT'S TIME OF DEATH, ONE SHOULD HUG THE DEATH TIGHTLY, AND TELL THE DEATH THAT I WAS WAITING FOR YOU TO REACH ME AND ONE SHOULD TELL THE DEATH THAT IT WAS THE BEST LIFE. **BECAUSE IT IS THE END OF ONE LIFE.**

CHAPTER TWENTY-FOUR

Named as Life

DAVE there are many stories in this world which are not meant to complete. Every story has its own purpose and meaning. Nature always gives a call when story is about to begin and about to end. And DAVE, when you have the knowledge. True knowledge about anything. Try to share & help other. Because you don't have to make friend whose vibes are matching yours, you have to make friend whose vibrations are not stable. You have to help them. And always observe that your friends are totally different than you, still you will have a great bond.

OPPOSITES ATTRACTS.

Many will understand and many will not. But you don't have to stop. You know that in this world many stories are just meant to be incomplete and broken. So I would say that just don't overdo anything in life. There should be everything in control. I have seen many people try to make themselves who they are not by doing treatments and changing their personality to impress other. DAVE this body doesn't belongs to you and always try to change, change should be the attitude of yours. A one should always remember that the body which is given to them is just for the temporary period of time, so it would be not wise to judge anyone. And never be the same person you used to be. Because the person who just want to be the same person who he/she was yesterday is nothing but still a child because everything starts from the basics but it should end in different manner from where it had started, the progress will always starts from the ground floor. But the tree must grow, because the seed cannot be a seed forever, an animal must hunt to fulfill its hunger, that animal can't be hungry the way it was yesterday. Just the way human age, from birth to death, the progress is always in the increasing level, same like a human must enhance his/her mentality. So no matter what so ever is your story, weather it is broken or incomplete, nothing is going to be achieved if you are still holding it. You knew that it will be useless. DAVE it should be let gone. Holding something is not going to make them go far away. Believe me holding anything is not going to help you with anything. It will hunt you forever. So rise and move on from every failure.

****

While travelling, I usually learn many things, like really many things. You see many different things, many different culture and main thing is that you listen to many different stories. Where ever you go, no matter how rich that country is and no matter how rich or poor a person is, the karmic cycle is always going to be the same for every individual. And as I am hermit and used to meditate, I have trained and evolve my mind, where I cannot have any interest in your lifestyle. I can feel anyone's vibration and chakra flows. I can feel your emotions, and can understand what you had done previously and what was bothering you.

MR. HERMIT are you any supernatural creature? And how do have any these powers.

DAVE, as I have seen human nature, they always want everything easily and quickly. But the thing is to reach somewhere you have travel through something deep. You cannot achieve something easily by just thinking that, you have to do something. You have to make an act while manifesting hard and by calming your mind. Whatever you want in life, always remember that you have to be patient and consistent to achieve that task.

As I said, I used to travel a lot, but in reality my wife used to travel a lot, she had travel the whole India and with daughter in law and son's support. Me and my wife even travelled to foreign countries. I said foreign countries. Can you even imagine that the person who has nothing in his life will travel foreign countries?

Literally I had nothing from the beginning, but I end up having all the possible this a human can dream of. I wasn't a billionaire or millionaire. I just have a heart to do things. I was really grateful to my supreme energy for giving me more than I actually deserves.

MR. HERMIT can you explain me about the theories and your perception about death.

DAVE why are you thinking about death while I am talking about my experiences.

Do you wanted me to die?

(MR. HERMIT was laughing and I have never seen MR. HERMIT laughing)

No, I was just curious Mr. Hermit, about death that's why I have asked you about the death, and I was really thinking about death because all you said about your experiences was not going to matter at last, because you are going to die anyhow. And what happens after death (I know there is no answer for after death, but tell me as per your knowledge). I just remember your previous saying about DEATH CAN BE HUGGED BY YOU AT LAST. Tell me something about recantation and stuff related to after death.

****

DAVE <u>after death</u> and <u>reincarnation</u> are two things which is beyond your imagination like many other things. But there is one thing certain about after life and that is YOU WILL PAY FOR WHAT YOU WILL DO. Life don't want you to do things which is illegal, illegal in the term for God not in terms of government. In every culture, there are many things that are considered bad and unholy, while in another culture they are basic necessities. But one thing is sure, everything is going to affect you in all ways, and god has created some situation for NOT the wellbeing of human. So God might have created you for the wellbeing for others. So you are supposed to do good deed and supposed to be knowledgably person and being useful to other human at time of your needed knowledge. According to God, killing animals is a punishable crime in some religions. However, people of the same religion might be born near the shore and work as fishermen. So, how do you know what is truly punishable? DAVE everything is planned in this world, maybe for supreme energy that fisherman is holier than that of a knowledgeable person. So for that I have no good explanation, but you have to control your emotion and always do good deed that is what I'll tell you about after death.

Reincarnation holds two element. Firstly, it involves the idea of being reborn into a new body, determined by one's deeds from previous and present lives. This concept suggests that our actions today can influence our future circumstances, connection to studying for a degree to prepare for a job. Just as pursuing education benefits future employment, our present actions shape our subsequent lives. However, unlike a selective course of study, life presents us with diverse experiences. Each individual is destined for a particular path, guided by what they are meant to do. While there may be aspects beyond comprehension, you've shared an essential elements, offering a foundational understanding of the concept.

MR. HERMIT I'll understand, I want to know more about this things.

DAVE you will understand it, believe me. Just be patient.

CHAPTER TWENTY-FIVE

The Lost Shoe

DAVE sometimes I think how the world is running. It is unknown to me whenever I try to understand and try to reach to its level.

Let me ask you that how is this chair besides you is created?

It is simple, it is made up from wood.

And where we get wood from?

Trees.

And how trees come to existence?

Maybe earth has evolve its tissues & fiber that converted into trees like substance, and after few years it become fully adaptable according to environment.

And how earth is created?

Maybe when gravity pulled the gas or particles and situated into a rock which was created by the crashing of meteor. And become third planet of solar system.

Nice try DAVE, now tell me how sun is created?

It's a rock which was made from hydrogen and helium gases with dust particles and it is something related with nebula.

Tell me how those gases are formed?

They were find in our galaxy, roaming here and there.

Funny, and tell me how galaxy was created?

Galaxy is part of our universe?

Then how universe was created or formed?

As per modern science and as well as ancient science there are multiple universes, and there are created by one god?

Then who created that one god?

Maybe the supreme god.

Then who created the supreme god?

They were just created.

DAVE that is the thing. We all had seen everything from the beginning, means we have seen everything from its basic form. Everything was made out of something, everything needs something to relay on. Humans are made of something (four gases and atoms). Cotton is made out of something, silk is made of something, and plastic is made from something. We all know that something is made from something. So when we try to understand how everything began, we run into a puzzle: if there was nothing before the supreme energy, what caused it to exist? It's like asking what caused the thing that caused everything else, and so on till infinite. It's hard to grasp how something can come from nothing, especially without any space or time for it to happen in.

This mystery pushes us to rethink what we know about reality. Maybe the answer lies in the very nature of the supreme energy itself, something beyond our understanding. And that is what irritates me every time when I think of it. *The theory of nothing.* The more questions raises the more answer from different path you will get. DAVE **life is so magical than you expect.** If you know nothing about the question and never thought of it, just remember that life has its magic. So let the life do its magic.

And DAVE from the word magic, I recall a story. Story of my grandson.

****

MR. HERMIT. You had a grandson? How amazing. (Wait, so at what age did MR. HERMIT becomes the official MR. HERMIT? Is he immortal, or his son had early marriage? Let the story continues, let MR. HERMIT complete everything first, because I have started thinking that he a superhuman.)

My grandson had many a fantasies, he was born with a creative mind and with a good humor like me. And I forget to tell you about my grandson. He was born after one year of my son marriage. And he tells me stories which I finds sometimes realistic and connected to something. He don't have physic abilities. But I felt like he was trying to connect the connected things. <u>Let me tell you one last story.</u>

When he was 5 year old, he told me a story, a story of his magical trip. As our relatives and all the family members have to attain our family function, I and my wife decide not to go and let our son handle this time. So they all went, my son and my brothers' sons with their wives in one car. It was visiting a temple after rebuilding it after 60 years. During this visit, there were special ceremonies and rituals to celebrate in the temple's restoration. They all have to go to a desert. Practically the place is situated in a desert where resources were very limited. It was a desert where our bloodline begins. And if I describe you the scene of there and its weather. It become the desert basically for few years, and then the land converts into an ocean. And the temple which I am talking about is situated in the middle portion. I have to say that the ancient architects were so brilliant when it comes to convert any land into a habitable land. They have the pure knowledge and they do it in a very well manner because there was no politics during that time and no sub branches and middleman to corrupt. They have to do properly because of the fear of kings.

So they all were going to that temple which was 500km away from my home. A long way. And the air of that place was salty so purchasing vehicles can be rough at there. As I said it is not completed desert, it has places which is partly forest. But as it was mostly covered with that desert part. They all were going there where the population count is merely 50,000 at that time, (I don't know today's scenario, because is now converted into a business and industrial place and become a tourist attraction because it has many a good monument and has ancient architecture).

I used to go there every year and my legacies was also doing that, me and my wife used to go there once a year and during our time there was totally less developed transportation and more damaged roads, at our time situation is at its worst condition, but we used to go every once a year. So that was where they are heading and during that time there was no hotel and rest rooms so my son and his participants had stayed at our relatives' house. And during that time house were built from mud. So basically it was fully surviving 2 days and for the younger generation it's hard to live without fan. And during those two days when the temple was being decorate because of the God festival (I am talking about the temple which was situated in the forest region). All of the members were working for temples decoration, they all were present during that time and for children. Children were always in their own fantasies.

They all were playing hide and seek, and there were so many children that, if even someone is lost. It was going to be hard to find and that was what happen. My grandson had a same habit of exploring abandoned places like my wife, so in the name of hide and seek he went to find something amazing, he wants to find something new so he started roaming. And in search of nothing he lost the track like it happens in movie. When he started panicking and crying, he found an abandoned temple, and that temple was in height so my grandson started climbing while fear rolling from his eyes. It wasn't challenging so he climbed there and it was really abandoned, like the nature was really connected with the temple branches of trees and weed had grown inside the temple interior. And as a children you really don't have fear of anything except height and loud noise. So he went inside of the temple for seeking some help, and he fined two guy, two guy with very less things with them, they were poor people or thieves hiding there. Because normally in human mind this kind of things come naturally to judge someone in the worst possible way, but I find out that they are something different. My grandson told me that they both asked him very kindly that: are you lost?

And then they watched something in a transparent cube, a transparent cube shows them that his parents are doing lunch with our relatives and they all are sited in a lined position and they both tells them the way, and when he was coming back towards the reaching point and whenever he becomes confused he initially becomes confident and heard the two guys voices in his mind and after reach towards the point where he left off. He hugged his father and cried, after asking the reason he told them that he was lost and two guys help them find way and he lost his shoe while reaching back. None of that have doubted anything because they all knows that children connects everything with something. And after coming back home my grandson told me that story while we are going to temple which was nearby our home. I also thought that it was a dream but what if it was not?

(After 2 year)

When we returned to the spot where the temple once stood, my grandson insisted on showing me the way. As we arrived, I was surprised to see that the temple was indeed there, just as he described. However, it wasn't as grand as he remembered. He pointed out that it seemed smaller and without a roof, suggesting it might have collapsed during its time submerged beneath the ocean. Despite its diminished state, the remnants of the temple still held a sense of ancient majesty, with weathered stone walls bearing testament to its former glory. We imagined how it must have looked in its prime arc, towering and resplendent against the skyline.

Seven years later, upon revisiting the area, we found it transformed beyond recognition. The once serene site of the temple was now a bustling hub of industry, with factories and warehouses sprawling across the landscape. Where the temple once stood, there was now a modern structure, likely housing machinery and equipment for an automobile factory. I thought that why it was not preserved? Because old heritage can be used as tourist attraction.

Thinking back on the temple's fate, I feel a twinge of nostalgia for the time when it stood proudly in its tranquil surroundings. Its transformation reflects the unstoppable progress, reminding me of how the world changes over time.

But whenever I think about my grandson's childhood, this thought that pushes me and it holds a special place in my heart, marking the beginning of his many adventures. As he grows older, I'll cherish the memories of this tale and the questions it raises. Who are those two guy? What was that cube my grandson was talking about? And what is connected with that shoe or it was just a random fall out? Was it his dream? How did they find that cube if the story was true?

That story was never been mentioned as time goes by, I think now even my grandson has forgotten that story of his. I think that many a times we do have experience many supernatural things but we have no reliable proof for that and as the time pass by we only feel the mirage of that ideology or event.

WE USUALLY FORGET THINGS BY COUNTING THEM AS FICTIONAL THINGS AND THOUGHT OF IT AS USELESS THINGS.

BUT, THOSE ARE THE WAY YOU ARE CONNECTED TO SOME KIND OF SUPERNATURAL ENERGY.

CHAPTER TWENTY-SIX

Illusion for Reality

DAVE the bond between the grandparents and grandchild were always on another level, that bond is greater than the bond a child have. And do you know DAVE the more you know about the world the more you get confused weather to live or die. Because after having the spiritual knowledge, a person is nearly dead (mentally) from this world, he was alive in different voidness. And if you don't know anything about the mysteries and creation it doesn't going to matter because you are still going to live the fullest if you have a healthy mindset. Just think those who don't know about anything whatsoever are also living, early awakening, going to job, business or profession, having lunch, spending family time, dancing, playing, travelling and sleeping. They do not know and not even interested into learning the different part of life. They just wanted to make their life worthy. When I started seeking knowledge, I found nothing. Even when I was ignorant, I found nothing. So tell me what is the difference it makes about knowing the stuff and not?

What difference does it takes?

I am not sure MR. HERMIT but having knowledge has improved me as it gives a vast thought process. Whenever something bad will happen it is not going to make me sad which it used to make me before, I think materialistic things will not draw my attention. No human is going to attract me by their beauty because it is just external, true beauty lies inside, even a masculine person can look bad if he has no sense of speaking in manner, no etiquettes and zero smartness. Physical health & mental health are necessary. Because with proper knowledge one can be physical fit. So no matter what a person is doing, they should know its full potential of understanding. Because:

A ONE SHOULD NEVER STOP LEARNING, BECAUSE LIFE NEVER STOPS TEACHING.

******

(*Night time*)

We both were sleeping and suddenly I asked MR. HERMIT a question which I want to ask him for so long. So, MR. HERMIT it's been how many years since you have moved to here and how you reached here. I am asking this because in your story your grandson was also born so basically you have reached 60 years in age approximately, and you are in your 80s if I am not wrong. But you have told me that you have many stories of your grandson. So it concludes that you with him for long. And you are in some different level from a human, so how you have achieved that in a very short period of time?

After I asked the questions, I started hearing the snoring. It means two possible things.

I am talking to myself or MR. HERMIT fooled me once again.

I then started thinking about my parents. Because night is the time where you can be real with yourself and besides it's been very long since I am here and now I am bored like hell. And I do think this been a month now. But the thing is that, why my parents had not reacted much when I was no more with them and it was going to be a month now. (My doubts are raising about everything which was going since last month.) I really do think that something, maybe something is connected with everything which is going on here.

What is going on is beyond my imagination after the things MR. HERMIT has taught me. I am trying to connect everything which he has told me from the beginning. I am trying to reach to the hidden message

Am I in a dream?

OR

Am I connected to a different dimension?

Everything is so messed up, let me do something next morning. But for now, (as per MR. HERMIT everything is just an illusion, so I would like to sleep tensioned free in this illusion). And apart I am not even able to do anything right now even If I wanted to do.

(Next morning)

MR. HERMIT I want go home today, to check whether everything going right or not, what will happen if my parents had thought of me as kidnapped or lost somewhere. And Mr. Hermit, is my parents connected to you?

DAVE, everything is connected. Every being in this world is connected, connected to fulfill their duties through others help. So you may go after completing the story.

So where were we last? Yeah, grandchild of mine. I have lived my life to the fullest and I don't have any regret of my life. <u>I don't know when I will die from this existing life because I am beyond your imagination.</u> But I am ready for every challenge which will occur and life thrives on me. And DAVE.

You have fully experienced life in your past..... You are free from messenger now.

Dream is Gone

A silence is spread across the park. I felt like the mistaking words flowing from the mouth of a stranger. A sickness going through the vein of mine before the generalized outcome can be heard from the disease. I was still sitting in the park and the moon has shown its gigantic shape while blooming the surrounding. I was seeing few people roaming in the park and kids still playing.

My eyes were opened. I was not in panic. I was in the war with my thoughts. What I have experienced? What I just dreamed in an almost blink of an eye?

I was loosing few insights. This happens in a pattern. Every time when I want to remember something from my dream I always forgets it. But I will try to recall and starts writing every foggy dream I remember and I will CONNECT to dots behind the dreams.

The brain had started to connect somewhere. Somewhere I am unaware of. The lessons which the spirits wants to teach me. The way they generate the story. The co-relation of the connection and the ability of the drawn and to conclude with the voidness by forgetting the chronology always has put the answer in the sequential manner.

(After few heavy thoughts)

I went straight towards my home. I started walking while observing the surrounding. A person with fantasy exists in the realm of their imagination. Sometimes they reveals the secret of something which was never heard by anyone through their internal connection.

(Next Day)

Hello DAVE. How are you? It was a good day I have spent with you yesterday. And I am looking forwards to have such meets with you. Hoping you don't mind.

(Yesterday and Today.
Nothing in between.)

Yes LUCY it was a great day with you. And I would like to go on the top of the hill which I have seen in the middle of the way coming all the way down to my home. Do you have any idea about that biggest hill?

Yeah. We will surely go. And don't tell anyone about that place. We will go there. It's my favorite place because no human contact will be there. I often used to go there with my family and father. It's our secret picnic spot.

I was shocked hearing that.

I received an unexpected call from my father, who urgently needed me to send some documents, specifically income statements, from one location to another. Given my father's profession in banking, it's not unusual for me to assist in transferring files to our relatives.

Despite being in a lecture, my attention was solely devoted to my creative work - writing and sketching. These endeavors are deeply meaningful to me and are recognized for their distinctiveness and popularity in my own mind.

I was seeing LUCY who was focusing on the lecture. Where I also see the other classmate of mine who were focused in the lecture. But sometime when I see their attention snap. I thought that they all are just faking themselves.

Everyone is just into their own lost space where they find comfort until MORING HAPPENS.

Many of us experience dreams that we ultimately forget upon waking every morning. This forgetfulness often stems from wakening of our spiritual connection with the world around us, which remains largely mysterious and unfamiliar. As a result, we may fail to recognize the deeper meanings or messages that our dreams are attempting to convey.

The thing which I had fantasize in my past life story or the alternate integral story of mine through a messenger.

But now I understand that every story in this universe is mine. I am in every human being. We are the art created by the same hand. We are the creation. Spirits are also me, energy is also me. The sun and moon is also me. The universe is me. I am the particle and I am the atom. I am the whole creation and I am the galaxy.

(The thought changed and the progress created. The outcome become clear and path become free. I will grow, hope not for materialistic possession but to seek the ultimate truth.

Whispers From Above

As per our schedule. We went to that hill. We started climbing with our backpack on. I was neither happy nor sad while climbing. Dreams are an integral part of me. It's been a week since I had that dream and I still remembered the lessons.

We climbed towards the peak encountering the Danger board which was created by LUCY. And I found out that LUCY used to come here and she hides a bag behind the Danger board. She usually hides her things like books, sketches etc. Which she wanted to gift to nature and for those future person who is going to visit that mountain/hill often. She wants to leave a secret message and wants someone to find it.

I also haven't seen that thing. She just told me and I listened. While climbing I am enjoying the moments of Déjà vu. I was not aware of this place while being aware of it at the same time.

While climbing, Lucy told me the hidden things which she had buried and put at an isolated place.

(I just hope she isn't a Witch.)

After a few miles of walking. I was finally where I am supposed to be.

I am standing on the top of the hill. Exhaling the fresh air. Seeing the beauty of the imagination. Imagination created by an artist who is above us. Seeing us and waiting for us.

About Author

Dave Manav

I'm a 20-year-old student and aspiring writer, delving into the world of Fiction.

I am from Gujarat, India. I've been captivated by story writing since my early years.

Despite the demands of student life, I want to gift my Grandfather a present on his birthday which is on 29th May. I want him to know that your story will not fade away because your presencde will always exists in a book.

My writing journey has seen me penning diverse tales, with my novella **Celestial Whispers** standing as a testament to my dedication. Currently navigating the realms my creativity.